T
Great
Deep

Michael M. Middleton

For all those who yearn for "The Great Day".

At End of Day

Still I lie
in cool grass
soft and green;
bathed in golden rays
at end of day,
tranquil... content...
hedged by Hands unseen.

Michael M. Middleton

from *Sacred Journeys*
copyright 2002

Chapter One

Evening has come. William Thornton rises from his all too comfortable chair with a slight groan and turns off the television. "...news is as depressing as ever," he mutters as he switches off the set. "There's got to be something good going on somewhere! But you'd never know it... It seems to me that everyone thinks that the only good news is bad news!" he chuckles to himself. Turning to the far corner of the room, he asks, "Isn't that right, Zeke?"

The yellow and green parrot perks up and pertly replies, "You know it! Right on!"

William chuckles and stands to his full height. Placing the palms of both hands firmly against his lower back, he entertains a satisfying stretch, accompanied by a chorus of "Oh! Oh! Oh... that feels good!" Stretching one stiff ankle, he grimaces over the number of 'cracks' that it makes. "These poor old bones..." he muses.

Zeke chatters, "Silly old man! Silly old man!"

William chuckles again and then lets out a small sigh, clears his throat, and walks to the kitchen. A slight squeak announces the opening of the cupboard door and out of nowhere, a silver-gray cat appears.

"Well, good evening, Lucinda!" he says in a bright, cordial tone. "I see your ears are as sharp as ever. I never knew any cat that could hear a cupboard squeak from as far away as you! Yep... practically psychic! Darn near a miracle!" Stiff fingers caress the cat's luxuriant form, as she eagerly purrs in anticipation of dinner. "You old motorboat!" William chides.

Pulling open a drawer, he removes a can opener and opens a can of *Grilled Tuna Dinner.* Leaving the can opener on the counter, he places the opened can on the floor next to the front door. "Now be a good girl and eat all your dinner, if you want dessert!" he quips, feigning castigation.

Dessert always consisted of the same thing... a Maraschino cherry. William doesn't remember how he had discovered that she liked them, but Lucinda relishes them above any other treat. This gray cat has one serious sweet tooth!

William straightens up, twists the pewter colored doorknob, and pushes open the heavy wooden-plank door. He steps out onto the covered patio, which faces the long driveway leading out to Interstate 17. Leaning against the heavy wooden beam handrail, he soaks in the fading embers of a spectacular sunset. Hues of pumpkin and rose enflame the lower portions of a few feathery clouds as they chase the rapidly fading twilight. He draws in a long, full breath of the warm evening air, perfumed by honeysuckle and lilac, and says, "Mmmm...beautiful job, Lord."

The crickets and the bullfrogs are well into their nightly songs as he steps back and settles into a willow chair. It creaks and chatters a bit, but is still as solid as the day that he built it, some fifteen years ago. Gazing out towards the growing darkness, his eye catches a distant blue-white flicker. A few seconds later, other flashes follow; some on the lawn, a few from the trees, and still others dance in mid-air.

"Fireflies!" he says. "First ones I've seen this year!"
He grins to himself and shifts his weight to one side. Reaching into his pocket, he withdraws a small drawstring pouch. He pinches open the mouth and carefully pours a few pebbles into his hand. He selects one specific pebble, which looks like a small bead of crystal-clear glass, and returns the others to the bag. "I'll show you some shine!"

As he pinches the tiny glistening stone between his thumb and index finger, it erupts with a blinding, brilliant light… a living, liquid light far brighter and far whiter than anything known to man could produce. It blazes in a light so brilliant and so fluid that it leaves no shadow, but envelops all in its path. Bathed in this brilliance, the haggard old man becomes swallowed up in the memories of youth. The aches and pains of age dissolve as the ageless, timeless spirit within transports him to another time and place.

Chapter Two

It was the summer of William's twelfth year. An extraordinarily average looking pre-teen boy, he had slightly wavy medium brown hair and a fine, clear complexion. A sparse spattering of freckles were distributed across his face and arms in a wholly random fashion. All of his life up to this point, he and his family had lived in a comfortable little single level home in Reno, Nevada.

His father, Jacob Thornton, was a professor of chemistry at the University of Nevada. He was a man of average height, but extraordinary build. Despite being on the downhill side of middle-aged, he was as solid as a brick wall. He had been an all-American football player in college and looked like he could still compete on that level, if he chose to. He had chestnut-brown hair with a light peppering of gray and kept a neatly trimmed beard. His eyes were a deep olive-green. Unfortunately, they were usually obscured behind thick glasses, as his eyesight had dramatically diminished over the past several years. This was his one outstanding physical shortcoming.

William's mother, Theresa, was of a much slighter build. She was quite literally the skinniest person William knew. She was somewhat shorter than Jacob, with red hair and brilliant blue eyes. She liked to joke that, along with her exceedingly pale skin, this made her the most patriotic person in town!

William took delight in answering her with "Yes, Mother Theresa!" whenever she got serious about telling him to do something. This amused him, but did not have the same affect on her. Luckily, he had a visual 'early-warning' system. When her ears began to turn red, he knew that he had better not push it any farther.

Before William was born, Theresa had been a junior high school English teacher. Now, she worked at home as a freelance writer. She took on a wide variety of writing assignments including textbooks, nature guides, promotional fliers, advertising copy, and topical articles for magazines and newspapers.

She particularly enjoyed writing children's books and occasionally had success with science fiction short stories. She always seemed to be busy and the "tack - tack - tack -- tack-ding!" of her typewriter was seldom silent for long. Most nights, William fell asleep to its staccato lullaby.

William had one sibling, an older sister. Her name was Leslie. She was twenty-three years old and lived in Los Angeles. She was of medium height, with long, auburn hair and hazel eyes. She had always wanted to be a fashion model, but was repeatedly told that she was too short and didn't have 'the look', whatever that meant. William thought that this was crazy, although he'd never admit to thinking so. He still clung to the 'girl germs' mindset, at least outwardly.

Anyway, when her dreams of modeling hit rock bottom she did what was, in her mind, the next best thing. She took some graphic design and commercial art courses at a community college and landed an apprenticeship as a set designer. She traveled with a small team designing and building sets for fashion shows. They also occasionally took special jobs building seasonal displays for major department and clothing stores. One year, she had actually helped put together the Christmas display at *Macy's* in New York City. This put her on cloud nine all the way up to Easter.

Although Leslie's dreams of being a model never materialized, she was satisfied that she was 'still in the industry', as she put it. She tried to make it home to visit during the holidays each year and occasionally had the opportunity to visit at other times. Whenever she was traveling anywhere in the general area, she would do her best to drop in for a day or two.

This was one of those occasions. Leslie had several days off between jobs and had flown in to help the family pack. For the first time in William's life, his family was moving. William's grandfather had passed away three years ago. He and his wife, Mary, had owned a horse ranch outside of Rock Springs, Arizona for over thirty-five years. This is where William's father, Jacob, had grown up as one of eight children. He and his brothers and sisters had a nearly ideal childhood, growing up on a horse ranch in a log cabin.

Well, "cabin" wasn't exactly accurate… although that's what they called it. This cabin had seven bedrooms and four bathrooms. It was originally built as a typical three-bedroom, two-bath, but the couple's generous supply of offspring made several successive additions necessary.

Luckily, they could afford it. William's grandfather Seth didn't just raise horses; he raised thoroughbred racehorses. He seemed to have an unusual knack for this and many of his horses enjoyed outstandingly successful careers. Seth was somewhat of a legend in the horse racing community and made a very good living. He passed away a few years after declaring himself "semi-retired" and selling off all but a few horses.

Mary had done very well by herself, until recently. She still rose just before dawn most mornings and usually did a full day's worth of work before lunch. However, she had recently begun to experience erratic fluctuations in her blood pressure. This caused her to have blurry vision and bouts of dizziness, as well as occasional fainting spells. Medication improved her condition somewhat, but she was told that she could no longer drive and was under official medical orders to "take it easy".

When it became apparent that she would need help, Jacob offered to move back home. Of the eight children, he lived the closest and was financially and otherwise the most able to make the move. He also welcomed the opportunity to live in the country again. He looked forward to bringing up his son with the family-farm experience.

He landed a position teaching chemistry at Northern Arizona University in Phoenix. With the exception of a few orientation meetings, he would be off most of the summer. He didn't begin teaching until the fall term.

So, the Friday after William's school let out for the summer, he and his family finished the last of their packing, loaded their rental truck, and left for Rock Springs, Arizona. They could easily make the trip in two days, but planned on taking four. They wanted to see the Grand Canyon and a few other sights along the way. A couple of friends of the family took a long weekend in order to drive the moving truck out, so that Jacob, Theresa, and William could all ride together in the car.

William had always wanted to see the Grand Canyon, but just couldn't enjoy himself on this trip. Although the idea of living in the country appealed to him, he was depressed and angry over having to move away from all of his friends. Despite his natural curiosity, he didn't relish leaving behind all of the people and places with which he was familiar.

Catching his son's eye in the rear-view mirror, Jacob asked, "What's the matter, spud-monkey?"

William defiantly choked back a grin, forced himself to frown, and turned his gaze to the side window. "Nothin'..." he muttered. Searching the creamcicle sunset for a way to express the anger, fear, and grief he felt inside, he could find no help in the soft orange glow.

After a moment of knowing silence, his mother turned her head towards him and cheerfully offered, "We're spending the night in Flagstaff tonight. We can order pizza, if you like... or maybe Chinese?"

William remained silent, pretending to not hear her.

"Oh, sweetie... you always liked it at Grandma's place. I hear the school in town is real nice. I'm sure that you'll fit in just fine. You'll see." She trailed off, sadly aware that her words weren't really making a difference.

Jacob's eye suddenly caught a sign on the side of the road. "Ah... there's our hotel!" he said as he snapped on the turn signal. "We'll get a good rest tonight and drive the last hour or so tomorrow morning. I'm sure Grandma can't wait to see you. She'll probably have a big batch of her famous strawberry muffins waiting when we get there."

William just drew in a long breath, sighed, and shrugged one shoulder. "Whatever..."

Jacob turned into the parking lot of the *Hampton Inn* and pulled up to the loading area at the front door. "I thought we would stay somewhere nice tonight, after that roach hotel we ended up in last night!" Jacob quipped. "Besides, they serve breakfast right here in the hotel... a full spread. I stayed here during that conference last fall. William, could you run in and get us a luggage cart?" he asked. "William?... Hey, spud-monkey!"

"Oh! Yeah, yeah, okay," William replied.

Jacob pointed and said, "They're usually somewhere just on the other side of the reception desk; on the right, if I remember correctly."

"Yeah, okay..." William said, as he exited the back seat. He stretched his legs and waggled his head in an attempt to wake up a little. "On the right?" he asked.

"Yeah, should be," Jacob responded.

"Hey, little guy, don't fall asleep until we get to the room!" Theresa said. "And watch out for those lazy doors!" At the last hotel, the automatic doors were apparently out of order, and William had done a 'vertical spread-eagle' against the glass, to the great amusement of a seven year old girl watching from inside.

Jacob did what he could to restrain his snickering as William threw his best attempt at an 'evil eye' in their direction. This snickering erupted into a full-blown belly laugh, as William once again walked unsuspectingly into non-functioning automatic doors.

From just inside the doors, there came a muffled voice. "Oh! Geez, sorry about that!" said a tall man in a gray business suit. He quickly lunged forward and to his left and removed the briefcase, which had prevented the doors from sliding open. "You okay, young man?" he asked.

William said nothing, but just stiffened his limbs and walked briskly past. He hoped that the stranger caught a glimpse of the scowl on his face.

The man in the gray suit, noticing who he correctly assumed to be William's parents, turned towards Jacob and Theresa and sheepishly offered, "Sorry!" just as the doors slid closed again.

William made no reply to the desk clerk's greeting of "Good evening, sir!" He walked straight past the front desk and retrieved a luggage cart from the little side room where they were stored. "The LEFT, Dad! They're on the LEFT," he muttered to himself.

As he arrived back at the car, he knew something was up. The luggage was stacked neatly at the back bumper... normal enough... but Jacob and Theresa had mischievous looks on their faces and Jacob was holding something behind his back. Theresa began, "Hey sport! Before we head in, we figured there was something we needed to give you..."

"...for your own safety!" Jacob added, as he whipped out his old college football helmet from behind his back.

This time, sincere humor won out and William joined in the laughter.

Jacob, still snickering, loaded the luggage onto the cart and said, "Help your mom in with the luggage. I'll park the car and be right in."

William and his mother each took charge of one end of the cart and headed for the front doors of the hotel. This time, just to be sure, William stopped short. He stepped forward, waving one arm high in the air, and the doors obediently slid open.

"That's my boy! Good thinking," Theresa said. "Better safe than sorry... again."

They waited at the front door for Jacob. He came strolling in the front door, humming some non-descript tune, and bounced up to the front desk. He signed a couple of papers, paid with his credit card, and got a room key. "412," he began. "The elevator's down this way, at the end of the hall."

The elevator was on the left, and William had a considerable amount of difficulty getting the luggage cart to make the turn. "Maybe you could just pull it up the stairs..." Theresa jested.

Jacob helped him straighten out the leading end of the cart and pulled it into the elevator. Theresa and William joined him inside, as he pushed the button for the fourth floor.

After settling into their room, they decided on pizza for dinner. William had feigned a lack of appetite at lunchtime, as some sort of a meager means of lashing out, and was famished. The pizza simply took control of his twelve year-old frame as he wolfed down half of it by himself. The cheesy, greasy mess worked its magic and his mood brightened a bit.

After a little television and a nice, hot shower, William brushed his teeth and changed into his pajamas. He took a long, hard look in the mirror and thought about what he was leaving behind… and wondered about what was to come.

He definitely had mixed feelings about this move. He really did look forward to living in the country, especially in a log house. And it would be nice to see his grandmother and ride the few horses she kept around for old-time's sake.

However, he was keenly aware that he was leaving behind some long-standing friendships, and wouldn't know anyone at his new school. He had never been 'the new kid' before and did not look forward to being treated as he had seen other new kids treated. He had never had to start over like this before, and didn't really know how to. Still, he knew that the move was for a good reason and he felt a little guilty about the anger he felt inside. But he was not yet willing to let it go.

Chapter
Three

William slept hard and long. Usually an early riser, it was nine-thirty when his father woke him from a sound sleep.

"Hey, spud-monkey! Wake up!" Jacob shook his son's shoulder as Theresa slid open the thick, dark curtains. A blinding light assaulted the room, falling directly across William's face.

"Hey...geez! What the..." William threw a pajama-sleeved arm across his eyes and let out an obviously irritated moan. "...what, ...where?" He had slept so deeply that he was somewhat disoriented when he first awoke. Remembering where he was, he said, "Oh, yeah... what time is it?"

"It's nine-thirty," answered Theresa. "Dad and I are all ready to go. We've been waiting on you to head down for breakfast. You'd better hurry up, before the early risers clean out all of the good stuff."

William yawned, stretched, and slid out from underneath the white linen sheets. He sat up, rubbed his face with the palms of both hands, yawned again, and plodded sleepily to the bathroom.

"Hey, buddy... better wake up," his father teased. "We don't want you walking into any doors today!"

"Let it go, dad..." William said flatly. He shut the bathroom door behind him and turned on the cold water in the sink. Splashing a double handful onto his face, he briskly rubbed the sleep from his eyes. He then removed his pajamas and changed into the clothes that he had laid out on top of his suitcase the night before. He brushed his teeth, combed his defiant, wavy hair, and packed all of his stuff into his suitcase. After one last stretch and yawn, he opened the door, picked up his suitcase, and walked out into the main room.

"That was quick... you hungry?" his dad asked.

"Yeah, kinda'..." William replied, restraining one last yawn. "Where's the luggage cart?"

"Out in the hall," his dad answered as he vigilantly scanned the room for any belongings which might get left behind.

His mother asked, "Are you sure you have everything, honey?"

"Yeah, I'm sure," William replied. With some degree of effort, he flopped his suitcase on top of the stack already occupying the luggage cart. He had to lift it almost head-high in order to do so.

"I'll take the front this time," his dad said. "It steers easier that way."

Theresa was waiting at the elevator when they got there, and the doors slid open just as they arrived. There was a slight bump as Jacob lifted the leading end of the cart over the small lip and into the elevator. William helped swing the back end in and then pushed the button for the lobby. The doors closed and the elevator began its decent with a sharp jolt.

As the doors slid open on the ground floor, Jacob said, "You guys go ahead and get started. I'll take the luggage out and join you in a minute."

"Okay, Honey," Theresa said. "You want me to get you some coffee?"

"Sure, that'd be great," replied Jacob. "I'll just be a minute." He pulled the laden luggage cart past the reception desk and continued out the front doors.

Across from the reception desk, William and his mother found a full buffet line. There were numerous steam table trays full of scrambled eggs, bacon, sausage, ham patties, bagels, muffins, and pancakes. At the far end of the line, there were a variety of serving-size boxes of cereal in a big wicker basket, a large bowl of fresh fruit, and pitchers of milk and fruit juice. Just to the right of that stood a small table with coffee, hot water, and a basket containing a variety of tea bags.

"Wow!" Theresa said. "Looks great! Most places, you're lucky to get a muffin and a piece of fruit."

She and William loaded up their trays and picked out a table to sit at. After setting down her tray, she went back for Jacob's coffee.

William took a big sip of orange juice and quickly realized that he hadn't waited long enough after brushing his teeth. "Ugh!" he grimaced.

Just then, his mom showed up with the coffee for his dad and asked, "What's wrong, sweetie?"

"Toothpaste… orange juice…" he said.

"Oh!" she giggled. "Take a bite of eggs; that'll fix it." She glanced over her shoulder and said, "Dad should be here any minute." She sat down and began eating.

Moments later, Jacob arrived carrying a plate full of bacon and scrambled eggs in one hand and a huge chocolate-chip muffin in the other. His silverware protruded from his shirt pocket. "They were out of trays…" he said. "Oh, man! I'm famished." He sat down and began devouring his meal.

Following a hearty breakfast, they cleared their places and headed for the car. As Jacob squeezed himself behind the steering wheel, he said, "Ahhh! Oh man, I'm not gonna' need to eat for a week!"

"Yeah, right!" Theresa quipped. She knew that he would be 'famished' again by lunchtime.

Within twenty minutes of getting back onto the interstate, they saw the first sign for Rock Springs. "Hey! Hey! There it is! We'll be there in about an hour," Jacob said. "Are you doing okay back there, son?"

"Yeah, fine…" William replied. Despite his reservations about moving, he was looking forward to getting there for one reason… to get out of the car. This four-day car trip was the longest he'd ever taken and he didn't much care for it. *Whatever I do for a living when I grow up,* he thought, *it will definitely not be anything involving travel.*

During the next hour of travel, William studied his dad's reflection in the rear-view mirror. There was a growing glimmer in his eyes as they drew closer to Rock Springs. In some mysterious manner, William knew that his dad was reliving fond memories of childhood. He made a game out of trying to guess what it was that evoked these memories at any given moment. Whenever he noticed a sudden glint of recognition in his father's eye, he would quickly attempt to decipher what had evoked this unspoken flood of nostalgia.

At times, William was fairly certain that he had figured it out; they had just passed a diner or a campground or a prominent landmark of some sort. Other instances were more enigmatic. William thought back to all the stories that his dad had told him about growing up in this area--yet whatever had sparked a memory at certain points along the way simply eluded William's ability to discern.

Suddenly, William's train of thought was interrupted. Just as they crested a small rise in the road, his mother said, "Oh! There's our turn," pointing to an enormous weeping willow tree, about half a mile ahead on the left.

Jacob turned his head slightly and replied, "Yep! We'll be there in a few minutes." He flicked on the turn signal and began to slow down.

The family ranch was located about five miles east of Interstate 17. A lightly graveled dirt road wound its way back between rows of cottonwood, willow, and ponderosa pine trees. About halfway there, a concrete bridge crossed the Agua Fria River. Jacob pointed to his left and said, "...best fishing hole in Arizona, right there!"

Just at the point where the branches of two enormous maple trees formed a natural archway across the road, the ranch house came into view. A fence constructed from lodgepole pine marked the point at which 'road' became 'driveway'. Jacob pulled the car through the open gate and up to a row of hedges, which defined the edge of the lawn. He turned off the engine and said, "Pile out!"

A flagstone walkway led up to the front patio. This was a concrete pad, some twenty feet wide and six feet deep. It was surfaced with flagstone and covered by a cedar shingle roof. The corner posts, which held up the roof, were engraved with depictions of squirrels, raccoons, deer, and other forest creatures. On either side of the door stood three-foot tall wooden bears, which had been carved by a chainsaw artist. The bear to the right of the door held a sign which read "*Welcome, friends!*"

There was a note thumb-tacked to the middle of the wooden-plank door. Theresa reached the door first, removed the note, and read it aloud.

"Jacob and family, Go on in and make yourself at home. I ran into town to pick up a few things for dinner. I'll be back soon. So glad you're here! If you're hungry, there's soup in the crockpot and a plate of cornbread on the counter. Woulda' had strawberry muffins waiting for you, but I ran out of flour. I'll have them ready for breakfast tomorrow, I promise!"

Just as Theresa finished reading, they heard the distant clanging of a bell. Turning back towards the car, they saw a horse-drawn wagon in the distance. "No!" Jacob began. "She didn't! I don't believe it..."

Several hundred yards away, William's grandmother, Mary, was driving an old hay wagon down the dirt road. She was clanging a bell which was mounted at the front left corner and waving her broad rimmed hat high in the air.

"She went all the way to town in that?" asked Theresa in amused disbelief.

"Feisty old gal, eh?" Jacob chuckled.

A few minutes later, Mary pulled up in the wagon and parked it next to the car. She set the hand brake and called out to Jacob. "Well, what are you waiting for? Get over here and help your old lady down!"

As he made his way to the wagon, Jacob replied, "You don't exactly look like you need help, but I'll oblige; just for the sake of manners."

"That's a boy!" Mary said, as Jacob offered his hand to help her down.

Jacob embraced her and said, "Oh, it's good to see you, Mom. But what's the deal with driving that old junk-buggy all the way to town? When Theresa read the note, we just assumed that you had caught a ride with a neighbor."

Mary defiantly lifted her chin and waggled her index finger in the air. "The doc' said I couldn't drive a car no more... he didn't say anything about a wagon. Besides, if I have one of my fainting spells; Chester here is a good horse, he knows the way home." She paused a moment, and concluded with, "The only tricky part is crossing the interstate!"

She then motioned to William and Theresa, who were still waiting on the porch, and said, "Well boy, what's holding you there? Come give your wretched old granny a hug. And how is my son's lovely young bride?"

"Fine, good to see you, Mom," Theresa replied. She turned to William and said, "Honey, go give grandma a hug and help your dad in with the groceries."

William walked over and gave Mary a hug. He and his dad then carried in the groceries as she unharnessed the horse and led him back to the barn.

After lunch, William's grandmother informed him that he could have his pick of any one of five bedrooms. "Mine's the one there, at the base of the stairs," she motioned. "And your parent's room is the big one upstairs, all the way to the left. Besides those two, you can lay claim to any bedroom you like. Your stuff is all stacked in the game room at the back of the house... the room with the pool table."

She turned to Jacob and Theresa and said, "Oh! And all the boxes you had marked 'storage' are out in the tractor barn, okay? I told your friends that would probably be a good spot... better than the horse barn!"

"Yeah, that's fine," Jacob said.

"They put all of your other stuff in your room already... real nice folks," Mary continued. "I tried to give them a little bit of traveling money, as a small 'thank you', but they wouldn't take it."

"Yeah, they're funny that way," Theresa interjected. "We'll send them a card, with some gift certificates or something in it."

William decided on a downstairs bedroom to the left of the game room. It was fairly spacious, with a good-sized closet and he didn't have to carry his stuff very far. It also had its own bathroom and wasn't far from the kitchen. He and his parents spent the rest of the day unpacking. After a late dinner, they fell asleep to the aroma of freshly baked strawberry muffins.

Chapter
Four

William awoke the next morning well before sunrise. The sound of a rooster crowing caught his ear as he stretched and sat up to look out his bedroom window. It had been a warm night and he had left his window open a bit. The crisp, sweet air was perfumed with the scent of lilac bushes in full bloom. He swung the window open and leaned out, bracing himself on the wide sill.

His window faced east and he had a terrific view of the coming dawn. A few sparse, feathery clouds glowed an unearthly pink as a brilliant orange sheen graced the horizon. A couple of stars were still barely visible high up in the deep lavender sky and a thin sliver of moon hung just above the tree tops.

Far off to his left, he could see a thick covering of mist hanging low over the pond his dad had told him about. *...Bass and catfish* he thought. *I'll have to find my pole and get out there later on.*

He was fascinated by the way the morning breeze stirred and sheared the mist. It looked like a pot of soup, boiling in slow motion. Now and then, the breeze would stretch a portion of the mist into a long, thin filament. It reminded William of the time that he and his family had made salt-water taffy. One of these filaments broke free and began drifting slowly westward.

The rooster crowed again, shaking William from his trance. He shifted his gaze to the right. About a hundred yards in the distance, just beyond the small shed his grandmother used to store her gardening supplies, he caught sight of a chicken coop. "When did Grandma get chickens?" he asked aloud. The rooster crowed again as he withdrew, pulling the window closed behind him.

He climbed down from his bed and retrieved fresh socks and underwear from his dresser. He then picked out a shirt and a pair of pants from the closet and headed for the shower. He loved the convenience of having his own private bathroom. He set his clothes on the counter and took off his pajamas. He stuffed his pajamas into the laundry bag, which hung from a hook on the back of the door, and stepped into the shower.

He fiddled with the faucet handles for a moment, until he got the water temperature just right. It wasn't until after he'd finished bathing that he realized he didn't have a towel. They hadn't been unpacked yet. He turned off the water and reached out to where he was accustomed to finding a towel hanging. After a moment of confusion, the sudden realization hit him.

"Oh man!" he groaned. "Great! That's just great!" Tearing back the shower curtain, he looked around the room, considering available options.

Just outside the door were a couple of pillowcases full of miscellaneous odds and ends; shoes, toys, books, and such. Being careful not to slip on the wet floor, he deftly paced over and emptied these out onto the floor. As he did, he half-heartedly made note of where each item would be put away later in the day. Drying himself with the empty pillowcases, he stuffed them into the hanging laundry bag and got dressed. After brushing his teeth and combing his hair, he flicked off the bathroom light and walked out to the kitchen, eager for breakfast.

"Good morning, my boy!" Mary greeted him as he entered the kitchen. She was seated at a small wooden table in front of a large picture window. Morning sunlight filtered through the country blue curtains, casting an aqua glow across the room. She held a cup of coffee in one hand and a large book lay open on the table in front of her.

"Good morning, Grandma," William replied. "Whatcha' got there?"

Mary paused for a moment, then glanced down at her Bible. "Oh, this! I'm just doing my morning devotions. There's no better way to have a good day than to start it off with the good book!"

William pulled up a chair and sat down across from her. Noticing an old photograph laying off to the side, he picked it up and asked, "Who is this? Is that Dad?"

"No, sweetie," Mary replied. "That's your grandpa! I took that picture of him on our honeymoon."

"Your honeymoon?" William asked with a hint of both surprise and amusement in his voice. "But... he's sitting in a tent."

"Yes, dear," Mary replied. "We camped out on the Oregon coast... a beautiful spot near Coos Bay."

"You spent your honeymoon at a campground?" William asked in amused disbelief. "I thought that honeymoons were supposed to be at big fancy hotels in Hawaii, or something like that..."

Mary giggled and said, "Yes... well, I know that it probably sounds odd to you, but you know what an outdoorsman your grandpa was. And," she continued, "you know how fond of the ocean I am." She gestured towards the various ocean-themed décor that filled the kitchen. "So, you see, we had a real meeting of the minds. It was the perfect honeymoon, as far as we were concerned."

Setting her coffee cup down, she took the photograph from William's hand and lightly stroked it with her fingertips… obviously swallowed up in a sea of fond memories. Her mind returned to the present tense and she said, "Anyway, I keep this photograph right here, as my bookmark. That way, I get to visit with your grandpa every morning. One day, we'll be together again and I won't need this old picture anymore…"

William was grateful when the awkward silence was broken by the rooster crowing again. "Oh, yeah," he began. "Since when do you have chickens, Grandma?"

"I got them last fall," she replied. "Just a few weeks after you and your folks came to visit. I don't know… I just thought that it'd be nice to have 'farm fresh eggs' again, like when I was a little girl."

"So, do you get any eggs out of them?" William asked.

"Oh my, yes!" she replied. "In fact, it's somewhat of a problem. Those busy hens out there lay far more than I can use. I'm glad to have you and your folks here to help me use them up… probably still be more than we can use, though. I hate for them to go to waste."

William thought for a moment, and inquired, "Well, hey… maybe we could sell some of them?"

"You know, that's not a bad idea!" Mary replied. "How would you like a job?"

"Um, I don't know… I guess." William said.

"Sure," Mary continued. "You collect the eggs each morning and throw the chickens some feed. I keep it out in the garden shed. Give them a coffee can full each morning… I'll show you how."

"But who do we sell the eggs to?" William asked.

Mary replied, "I'm sure you can scratch up some egg business from the neighbors down the road. There's about five or six families within a short ride. As soon as you get a few dozen saved up, I'll take you around with the hay wagon and you can keep whatever money you make. Fifty cents a dozen is a pretty standard traditional price... at least 'round these parts."

"Well, okay," William said. "I guess I can live with that!"

"Of course!" Mary concluded. "A boy your age should have some pocket money he can call his own. And putting in a little work for it just sweetens the pot."

Just then, William's stomach rumbled loudly and he remembered how hungry he was. "What's for breakfast, Grandma?" he asked.

Mary raised an eyebrow, leaned in towards him, and matter-of-factly asked, "How do you like your eggs, boy?"

The smell of breakfast cooking woke William's parents. They soon joined William and Mary at the dining room table. This was a heavy wooden table, crafted from old railroad ties. Jacob's father had hand made it when Jacob was a boy. It was inlayed with relics of the old west... horseshoes, railroad spikes, spurs, and the " business end" of several branding irons. A strand of barbed wire formed a decorative border all the way around, about three inches from the outside edge. All of these various elements were set into depressions, which had been chiseled and gouged into the heavy wooden beams, so that they were flush with the top surface of the table. A thick coating of glossy polyurethane sealed everything in place.

Jacob entered the room first. "Mornin' Ma', you got the vittles on?" he asked in a mock country twang.

"Hey, don't sass me, boy!" Mary replied in a jovial tone. "I can still take the strap to ya'!"

Entering the room, Theresa said, "I tried that… it doesn't help. The only thing that works is to starve him."

"Well, I'm afraid that won't happen here!" Mary replied.

The table was spread with plates of eggs, bacon, ham, toast, and the strawberry muffins she had baked the night before. "Yep, you still set quite a table," Jacob said.

"Well, when you spend half your life cooking for a mob of youngsters," Mary began, "It's kinda' hard to break the habit."

After breakfast, they all decided to take a stroll around the property. Mary relished the opportunity to show off the improvements she had made since the family last visited. She pointed out the minor repairs she had made on the tractor barn and the horse barn. These stood side by side about a hundred yards north of the house. A bit farther to the east stood the hay barn. A large wood shed stood just a few paces from the northeast corner of the house.

As they walked south along the back side of the house, Mary pointed out the various sections of flower garden. As they came to the southern end of the house, she gestured and said, "…And there's my little vegetable patch." This was somewhat of an understatement. It looked more like a small farm to William. It was several times larger than their old yard back in Reno. A miniature white picket fence about two feet high formed a tidy border around the outside. Rows of corn and okra ran east to west at the far end, filling about half of the area. The remainder of the garden consisted of large mounds of dirt where squash, pumpkins, and watermelons grew. There were also standing wire structures, which supported plantings of tomatoes, peppers, and beans. A separate raised bed in the northwest corner contained plantings of what she referred to as "root crops"… potatoes, carrots, radishes, and onions.

"My goodness, Grandma! You trying to feed Poland, or something?" William quipped.

"Well, you know how your granny likes to garden," Mary replied. "Once you've got the bug, you just can't shake it."

"But what are you going to do with all of it?" Theresa interjected. "I mean, we'd like William to eat more vegetables and all, but I don't think we can swing this!" she giggled.

"Well, I do plan on canning a lot of what we won't use right away," Mary explained. "And then there's this group from a big church in Phoenix. They'll come and harvest anything green thumbs like me want to donate. Then, they take it around to street missions and food banks... stuff like that. This little vegetable patch is going to help out quite a few needy folks. They call the program 'Gardens for God'... I like that. Anyway, that there's the shed where I keep the chicken feed, William." She motioned to a storage shed about eight feet wide standing just outside the eastern edge of the garden. "And that," she pointed off to the left a bit, "...is the chicken coop. Ought to be obvious, even to city folk like ya'll." She copied Jacob's mock country accent from before breakfast.

Glancing off to his left and noticing a large assembly of cattle in the distance, Jacob asked, "So... I see that you decided to lease out the big pasture again this year?"

"Oh, yeah," Mary answered. "The Phillips down the road a ways are going to summer a few dozen head here. In exchange, they're going to keep the horses fed and watered for me. And," she continued, "I get a chest freezer full of beef when they go off to market this fall."

"Sounds like a deal to me!" Jacob said. He paused for a moment and continued, "Well, by the way they're all bunched up there, I'd say they found the blowhole."

Mary replied, "Yep! Didn't take them long at all."

"*Blowhole*... what's that?" William inquired.

"Oh, it's a... well, a hole in the ground..." Jacob began. "It's a small opening... a tube of sorts, connected to an underground cavern."

Mary continued the explanation where Jacob left off. "You see, some of these openings connect to caves which have other, larger openings some distance away. Changes in temperature and air pressure create a natural flow of air, which is quite noticeable at the smaller openings. A nice, cool breeze blows out of them. It's Heaven for cattle on a warm day. Many times, they'll even prefer it to a shady tree."

"Really... there's caves around here?" asked William.

"A few," Mary answered. "Just one here on our property, that we know of...' *the fort*.'"

"*The fort!* I'd forgotten about that," Jacob interjected. Seeing the question in William's eye, he explained, "It's a little old thing. It opens up on the other side of that hill over there. It only goes back thirty feet or so, before it gets too narrow to squeeze through."

"Why do you call it '*the fort*'?" William asked.

Jacob answered, "Oh, we used to play back there a lot. We hauled some chairs and a card table down into it and kind of turned it into our little fort. We even drug an old couch down there, if you can believe it! We kept a stash of soda and jerky and various junk foods down there. It was a really fun hang out."

"Cool, can I check it out sometime?" William asked.

"Sure, just be careful climbing down in." Jacob began. " It only goes down about eight feet below ground level, but you've got to climb over some big rocks. Some of them are pretty loose and could shift on you. Just take it slow."

Mary interjected, "Actually, we think it's connected to the blowhole out there somehow."

"Why's that?" William asked.

"Well," she explained, "we had this dog once..."

"Flash..." Jacob chuckled.

"Yep, 'Flash'," Mary continued. "You see, this one time he got himself sprayed by a skunk. I guess he knew that he wouldn't be welcomed in that condition... after he'd been missing for a couple of days, the boys found him hunkering down in the fort. Later that day, your grandpa Seth and I were riding out in the pasture there and smelled that skunk stink wafting up from the blowhole."

"Oh... makes sense," William conceded.

After lunch, William and his parents spent most of the rest of the day finishing their unpacking. Theresa decided to put a vacant walk-in closet to use as her office. It was a little small, as far as offices went, but had good lighting and an outlet for her typewriter. It was wide enough for her to set up her small desk against the back wall. The numerous shelves and cubbyholes, which had once been occupied by socks, shirts, underwear, shoes, toys, and bathroom supplies, worked perfectly as a makeshift filing system. There was plenty of room for all of her office supplies, with shelves left over for books, knick-knacks, and a private "mail-processing center". She was fastidious in the records keeping related to her writing career.

William neatly stored away the former contents of the pillowcases he had used to dry off with following his morning shower. Before moving on to other unpacking, he made a point of asking his mom for a few towels. He folded them neatly and stored them in the cabinet under the sink. He then organized the rest of his bathroom stuff and returned to his bedroom.

After noticing several things missing, he located a few boxes of his belongings in the tractor barn. They had been accidentally taken there along with the stuff marked "storage". He used a wheelbarrow to carry them back to the house and completed his unpacking.

By the time he finished, he figured that it was too late in the day to go fishing at the pond, like he had planned to do. He decided that instead of hiking all the way across the pasture for maybe half an hour's worth of fishing, he would just leave early and make a full day of it the next day. Besides, he was kind of hungry and could smell dinner cooking. His mother had made lasagna, one of his favorites. Also, Mary had told him that she had some sort of a job for him to do after dinner.

After dinner, his grandmother informed him of his task for the evening. "Under the sink there," she began, pointing towards the kitchen sink, "...there's a whole case of mouse traps. I picked them up in town yesterday. I've been finding lots of signs of mice around lately, and would like you to scatter a few of those around."

William was actually somewhat squeamish about this kind of thing, but was proud to be trusted with the responsibility. "Sure, Grandma," he replied. "Where do you want them?"

"Oh, slide one behind the stove... between the refrigerator and the trash can... any of the cabinets with boxes or bags of food," She began. "While you're at it, put one or two out by the grain bags in the horse barn. I've found a few holes in them lately. You know how to set them without snapping your fingers, boy?"

"Yes, Grandma!" William replied, rolling his eyes.

"Well, smear a little peanut butter on the trigger to bait them... peanut butter works much better than cheese," Mary concluded.

William baited and set the traps in the house and then smeared peanut butter onto the triggers of two others. He borrowed a flashlight and carried these out to the horse barn. He soon found the grain bags and set the traps. He carefully set one of them on the floor behind the bags of grain. The other one, he placed next to an old discarded boot a short distance away.

He then closely examined the bags of grain. "Those don't look like chew-holes," he said to himself. "That looks like they were cut... weird."

He returned to the house and, after a little television, settled into bed. He again left his bedroom window open a little and fell asleep to the distant songs of the night. Coyotes, crickets, and owls provided a much better lullaby than the car horns, loud neighbors, and sirens he was accustomed to in the city.

William slept soundly for several hours before he found himself suddenly awake. Intuitively, he knew that some kind of a sound had woken him. Yet, he heard nothing except the same distant sounds which had lulled him to sleep. He yawned and sat up to gaze out of his window.

Far to the northeast he could see the faint flicker of lightning, but there was no thunder. He listened hard and could just make out the muffled tinkling of the large wind-chime which hung near the front door. *No, that can't be it...* he thought.

He turned from the window and searched the darkness of his room. The faint glow filtering in from the hallway nightlight gradually revealed a book, which had fallen from the top of his dresser. "Aha!" he said aloud. Satisfied that the mystery had been solved, he lay back down and closed his eyes.

But sleep would not return so quickly. A few seconds after closing his eyes, a strange scratching sound caught his attention. He sat up about halfway and again searched the dim room. He heard the faint scratching again and was able to vaguely locate its origin. It seemed to be coming from behind his dresser, which stood opposite him to the left of his bedroom door. *Mice...* he thought. *That sounds like a big mouse!*

The bedsprings creaked loudly as he swung his legs out from under the sheets and sat up fully. There was the sudden sound of scurrying and a dark blur shot out from behind the dresser. It seemed to dart in the general direction of the kitchen. "Yeah, go ahead... have some peanut butter!" he said.

As he lay back down, eager to return to sleep, a sudden thought disturbed him. For the minutest fraction of a second, the dark blur had been illuminated by the hallway nightlight. Details of the image that had at first registered subliminally now began to invade his conscious mind. *No...no, can't be. I must've been seeing things...* He reassured himself that the dim light and unfamiliar surroundings were playing tricks on his sleepy mind. Turning on his side, he closed his eyes and drifted back into a deep slumber.

Chapter
Five

The sun had already crept high into the sky by the time William awoke on Thursday morning. His little adventure in the middle of the night had taken a lot out of him. The first light of dawn would have awakened him, but he had drawn the curtains the night before.

The room, which had once been occupied by his uncle Don, was decorated in a rodeo theme. This included the heavy curtains, which were very effective in blocking out the morning light. They were made from several pairs of blue jeans previously worn by Charlie Davis. He was once a well-known professional rodeo star, who owned a few racehorses on the side. He had purchased two of these from the Thornton family ranch.

William's uncle Don was a big fan, so Charlie had donated several pairs of jeans for Mary to cut up and make into curtains for his room. William had heard this story from his uncle innumerable times and, although he didn't know Charlie Davis from Bugs Bunny, he still thought that it was "cool" that his curtains had once been worn by someone famous. There were a few back pockets randomly distributed across the curtains, which William now found handy for holding pens, pencils, small toys, and other miscellaneous items.

William was disappointed when he rolled over to look at his clock and realized how late it was. *I should have thought to set the alarm...* he grimaced. Popping out of bed, he walked to the bathroom. He brushed his teeth and got dressed, deciding to bypass the shower.

His grandmother Mary was standing at the counter refilling her coffee cup as he entered the kitchen. She noticed William out of the corner of her eye and turned to greet him. "Hey, there! Good morning, boy! Slept a little late today, eh?"

"Good morning, Grandma," William replied. Yeah, well... one of your mice woke me up last night. Except, well... I don't think that it was a mouse, exactly."

"What do you mean, dear?" she asked.

"Well," he began. "I only caught a quick look at it as it ran out of the room. It looked a lot bigger than a mouse, though." William tilted his head and stared off into empty space as he struggled to recall the details of his nocturnal visitation. "And, well, it didn't run exactly... it was more like a hop."

"It hopped?" asked Mary with a hint of sarcasm.

"Yeah, I think so... sort of like a little kangaroo... a kangaroo-mouse?" he asked in a confused tone.

"Oh! I know," Mary replied. "Actually, that sounds more like a kangaroo rat. We've got plenty of those critters, especially in the hills west of here. I've never seen one anywhere near the house, though."

"But it was really big," William continued. "And..." He was about to relay the stranger elements of his encounter, but thought better of it. "Well, it was really big!"

Mary replied, "Yeah, they can get pretty big sometimes. I've seen them nearly the size of a small rabbit once or twice. Strange for one to be around the house, though... they usually stay out in the drier, rocky country. And they do their best to stay away from people."

" So... it didn't end up in one of the traps?" William asked... glancing nervously around the room.

"Nope," she replied. "The traps are all vacant. Those little things wouldn't do any more than make it mad, anyway. The varmint probably just got curious to see who the new folks moving in were. Probably won't be back, but let me know if you see it again, okay?"

"Yeah, okay," William replied. "I'm just gonna have a bowl of cereal quick, and maybe pack a lunch, and then go fishing out at the pond, okay?"

"Sure, hon'. Your folks ran into Phoenix to do some business at the bank and pick up some household stuff," Mary began. "They'll be back this afternoon. I'll let them know where you're at if they get back before you do. Oh, don't forget to collect the eggs and all before you take off."

"Eggs! Oh, yeah. I'll do that first," he replied.

A doorway at the back of the kitchen opened to a small utility room, which doubled as a pantry. William retrieved his boots from the far corner and put them on. Opening the door which led outside, he stepped out, turned to his right, and headed for the chicken coop.

Along the way, he glanced to his left and noticed that the cows were once again huddled around the blowhole. *I'll have to get out there and see that,* he thought. *Maybe I'll drop a rock down it and see if I can tell how deep it goes.* He had seen somebody do this in a movie one time. *Journey To the Center of the Earth,* he recalled.

He was so preoccupied with these thoughts that he stumbled over the wheelbarrow which he had used to retrieve his missing boxes from the tractor barn. A split-second of confusion was quickly followed by fear and pain. He tumbled directly over the broad side of the wheelbarrow, first landing chest-first on the wheelbarrow and then doing a summersault. He did a head-over-heels flip, landing flat on his back. Apparently, he'd been traveling faster than he thought, in an unconscious effort to finish quickly so he could go fishing.

"Owww!" he moaned, between staccato, labored pants. The fall had knocked the wind out of him and it took him a moment to recover enough to stand. He straightened himself up and determined to remember to put the wheelbarrow away somewhere when he got back from fishing.

After regaining his composure, William continued on his way to the chicken coop. It was surrounded by a wire fence randomly strung with lengths of barbed wire, "...not so much to keep the chickens in, but to keep the raccoons out," as his grandma had informed him. He opened the gate, walked in, and latched it closed behind him. Upon stepping into the large wooden shack that housed a dozen hens and one very vocal rooster, he suddenly realized that he had forgotten to bring the empty egg crates that his grandmother had left out for him. Instead of going back for them, he decided to un-tuck his shirt and use it as a makeshift pouch. He checked every nest with one hand, placing each egg in the pouched shirt, which he held with his other hand.

When he'd finished collecting the eggs, he let himself out of the coop and again latched the wire gate closed. He walked to the garden shed and, using his one free hand, opened the door. He quickly noticed a plastic bucket hanging on the wall and transferred the day's collection of eggs into it. He left the bucket sitting in the shed as he returned to the coop with the daily ration of chicken feed.

Returning the empty coffee can to the garden shed, he retrieved the bucket containing the eggs. Since he had to pass by it again anyway, he decided to go ahead and move the wheelbarrow somewhere out of the way. He decided that next to the woodshed would be a good spot and moved it there.

He then returned to the utility room behind the kitchen. This is where his grandmother kept a small refrigerator, specifically to store the eggs. He retrieved two of the egg crates she had left out for him, placed the eggs in them, and stored them in the refrigerator. The refrigerator had four shelves. The bottom shelf was designated for the current day's collection of eggs. The next shelf up was for eggs collected the day before, and so forth. When a crate of eggs reached the top shelf, a dated sticker was placed on it. Eggs not used or sold within a week of reaching the top shelf were to be discarded.

William placed his collection of eggs on the bottom shelf and rotated each of the other crates up one shelf. He placed a dated sticker on the crate which he'd rotated to the top shelf and closed the door. Satisfied that this task was finished for the day, he returned to his room to collect his fishing tackle.

William opened his closet door. He slid the shirts that were hanging in the front all the way to the right and retrieved his pole and tackle box from the back left corner. He then returned to the kitchen. Instead of taking the time to make breakfast, he threw a few apples and carrots into a bag. He then located the last of the strawberry muffins, a leftover pork-chop, and a couple of boiled eggs in the refrigerator and added these to the bag, as well. *That should last me most of the day*, he thought. He exited the house through the utility room, carrying his fishing pole in one hand and his lunch bag and tackle box in the other.

William crossed the backyard and came to the barbed wire fence, which separated it from the pasture. He slid his tackle box and lunch bag under the bottom strand of wire and lowered his fishing pole over the top, allowing it to rest against the opposite side of the fence. Using both hands, he then spread the two middle strands of wire apart as far as possible and carefully sidestepped through. Grateful to not have been snagged, he retrieved his pole, tackle box, and lunch bag and headed off in the general direction of the pond. He couldn't see it from his current vantage point, but had a good idea of the right direction to walk. From his bedroom window he had seen a large pine tree, broken off near the top, standing just beyond the pond. This tree now served as his beacon.

The ground was rockier and more uneven than it looked to be from a distance and William stumbled several times as he hurried along. Suddenly, he recalled his grandmother's warning to watch out for cactus and decided to slow down. "Cactus can easily be hidden by even short clumps of grass," she had warned. "Watch your step... and look before you sit!"

He also recalled his father telling him on many occasions that, "Discretion is the better part of valor."

After a few more moments of walking, he spotted one of the "long-thorn devils" (as his grandmother Mary had called them) and was glad that he'd decided to slow down a little. *I would not want to trip and fall on that!* he thought.

After nearly twenty minutes of walking, William finally came to the pond. It was somewhat more than two hundred yards long and about sixty yards wide. There were clumps of reeds and cattails here and there, somewhat thicker at the far end. Several trees and a few large bushes were scattered around the perimeter.

As William scanned the scene, his eye caught a glimpse of movement. He looked closer, focusing his attention on a large bush along the eastern bank. He definitely saw something moving, but couldn't tell what it was. His curiosity aroused, he began to walk along the bank in the direction of the bush. When he got close enough, he could make out the tip of a fishing pole sticking out from the far side of the bush. Somebody was already fishing at his grandmother's pond!

William didn't know any of the kids who lived in the area, but assumed that it must be one of them. *Or, it could be a drifter...* he thought. *...or maybe a convict on the run!* (He and his family had passed a road cleaning crew from the state penitentiary on the day they arrived.) He recalled numerous scenes of escaped convicts fishing in old episodes of *The Andy Griffith Show.* He kind of realized that this was a silly idea, but couldn't imagine who else would be audacious enough to trespass on his grandmother's ranch.

He decided that it would be best to get a look at whoever was hiding behind the bush, before he got too close. He thought for a moment and came up with a plan. He would toss a rock just close enough to whoever was on the other side of the bush to startle them. They would, William assumed, stand up to see what was going on. That way, he could get a good look at this trespasser and still be far enough distant to make a clean get-away if they looked dangerous. And if it was just some kid who lived close by, he could claim that he hadn't seen them.

William carefully set his fishing pole, tackle box, and lunch bag on the ground and began to creep forward towards the bush. When he got within about thirty yards, he stopped and scanned the ground around his feet. Spying a rock just a little bit larger than a golf ball, he reached down and picked it up. He studied the rough stone, doing his best to calculate how hard he would have to throw it in order to cover the desired distance.

He took his best baseball stance, eyed his target, and flung the stone high into the air. It whistled softly as it settled into a perfect arch. As William studied the stone's curved path, it soon became apparent that it was destined to fall short of where he had intended it to. "Uh-oh!" he said through clinched teeth.

Half a second later, a high-pitched shriek shattered the morning stillness. Holding the side of her face, a girl who looked about his age popped up from behind the bush. She was dressed in blue corduroy pants and a yellow shirt with frills on the sleeves and collar. She had cherry-red hair and green eyes. Suddenly, it alarmed William that he was close enough to make out her eye color. There was obvious rage on her face, which intensified when her searching gaze found him. "Uh-oh!" he said again.

The red headed girl pounced from behind the bush and began covering ground at a rate that seemed unreasonable for her stature. "Uh-oh!" William said one final time. "I'm sorry! I'm sorry! I'm sorry!" he pleaded as she approached.

The girl retorted, "Not as sorry as you're gonna' be!"

In vain, William began, "But I...I...I..." He tried to dodge the girl's punch, but wasn't fast enough. It caught him squarely on the jaw, knocking him to the ground... as much out of shock as physical force.

"Come on, stand up! I'm not through yet!" the fiery vixen taunted.

William had never hit a girl before, but now thought himself capable of it. He lunged forward, attempting to stand to his feet. Unfortunately, he slipped on a loose rock and fell backwards again. This time, he fell directly on top of a prickly pear cactus. "EEE-YAIH!" he screamed in pain and terror.

He leapt to his feet with such vigor that he seemed to defy gravity... with three lobes of cactus firmly lodged in his posterior. He swung around like a dog chasing its tail in a vain attempt to see this new assailant, all the time whimpering in pain. The sight of this was simply too much for the red headed girl. She dropped her fists and burst into laughter.

"Shut up! Shut up!" William shouted in crimson-faced rage.

"You, uh, seem to have a little problem there," she snickered.

William bit off another "Shut up!" as he gingerly reached back, attempting to dislodge his thorny assailant. This proved to be a fruitless effort. Even if he could see the cactus, it was firmly lodged and he had no way of grabbing hold of it without injuring his hands.

The humor of the situation having satiated her anger, the girl now actually felt sorry for William. "Um, uh, sorry about punching you," she began. "But you know... what were you doing throwing that rock at me, anyway?"

"That was an accident!" he protested.

"An accident?" she retorted. "That was pretty good aim for an accident!" she continued, rubbing her cheek where the rock had struck her.

"Well, you were trespassing," William began. "I saw your pole sticking out there and thought that you might be an escaped convict or something. What are you doing on our land, anyway?" Although he still didn't like moving here and leaving his friends behind, he thought that claiming ownership would reinforce his case.

"I'm no trespasser!" the girl snipped. She was still snickering a bit at William's hopeless attempt to dislodge the cactus. "Grandma Mary told me that I could fish here any time I wanted to."

This caught William off guard. "Grandma? She ain't your grandma... she's my grandma!"

"Oh!" she said. "You must be Billy. Grandma... your grandma... told me a couple of weeks ago that you and your folks were moving out here. My name's Shari. I live just down the road a bit, on Cottonwood Lane."

"It ain't *Billy*, it's William!" he protested.

Glancing down at the cactus still protruding from his backside, she retorted, "I don't know... you look like a Silly-Billy to me."

William snipped back, "Well, that hair of yours makes you look like you're topped off with a big cherry! How would you like me to call you 'Shari-Pie'?"

"It's Sharon Stewart," she said flatly. "Come over here and I'll help you with your, uh, little problem." She motioned for him to follow as she walked back towards the bush. "Come on, I've got a pair of needle-nose pliers in my tackle box."

Drenched in humiliation, he shuffled along following Sharon to where her tackle box sat at the pond's edge. She unlatched the top and flipped it open. Searching the various compartments, she located her needle-nose pliers. "Now just turn around and stand still," she began. "This won't take too long."

The physical pain that William felt was nothing compared to the damage that was now being done to his ego. He slowly turned around, bit his lower lip, and stared up at the clouds. He winced hard as each of the three lobes of cactus were yanked out by Sharon.

"Almost done," she continued. "There's just a few loose needles left to get... There, that's about all I can see. If there's any little ones left, you can use duct-tape to get them out later."

William did his best to block out the mental picture that last comment created. "Um... yeah, well... thanks, I guess," he muttered. Still stinging a bit, he walked back and retrieved his fishing pole, tackle box, and lunch bag. He picked out a spot down the shore a ways from Sharon and decided to salvage what he could of the fishing trip. The spot he'd picked was close enough to the thick patch of reeds and cattails at the far end of the pond that he figured there would be some lunker bass hanging out nearby.

He stared out over the water. *Let's see... he thought, fairly clear water... probably six or eight feet deep...* He set his tackle box down, opened it, and began picking through the neatly sorted compartments. He selected a 1/4-ounce black and yellow spinner-bait and attached it to his line. Bracing his foot against a large rock, he cast the line as hard as he could parallel to the outer edge of the reeds.

Allowing the lure to settle slightly, he took up the slack in the line. When the line became taut, he jerked the pole slightly to start the lure's blades spinning and began to smoothly reel it in. Every so often, he twitched the line a bit.

After several unproductive casts, he picked a different spot and tried again. He tried reeling slower. It didn't help. He tried reeling faster... still no luck. Even changing to a different color of lure didn't help. He was considering trying a crappie jig or a grub, when he heard Sharon calling to him from her spot by the bush.

"Hey! Spinners won't do you any good this time of day... too hot. The big hogs are lazy when it's hot. Try the ol' worm and bobber. I've got worms, if you need one."

William shouted back to her, "It'll be a cold day down below before I let a girl tell me how to fish!"

William's ego took another big hit when she reached down and lifted a stringer laden with four or five of the biggest bass he had ever seen. He turned away, pretending not to see. He opened his tackle box again and considered what to try next. While he was pondering this decision, he suddenly became aware of his hunger.

Setting his pole down, he reached for his lunch bag. Opening the bag, he removed the pork-chop, an apple, and two strawberry muffins. After stripping most of the meat from the pork-chop, he tossed the bone into the pond and devoured the strawberry muffins. Wanting to get back to fishing, he decided to save the apple for later and returned it to the bag.

He again turned his attention to his tackle box. He spotted a crawdad crank-bait in the back of one compartment and thought, *Well, if they're hiding down deep in the weeds, this should get their attention.* Removing the spinner-bait from his line, he returned it to the tackle box. He then picked up the crank-bait; being careful to avoid the two large treble hooks. After adding a couple of small split shot to make it dive deeper, he cast out next to a grouping of lily pads.

His first two casts proved fruitless. On the third cast, however, the line lurched hard and veered off to the right. "Woo-hoo! Fish on!" he hollered. He was quite pleased with himself when he noticed Sharon turn her head to watch. However, his pleasure diminished somewhat as he grabbed the bass by the gill plate and lifted out of the water. It wasn't puny, exactly... but it still looked like it could be a light snack for any one of the fish he'd seen on Sharon's stringer.

Well, at least I won't be skunked, he thought. He put the bass on his stringer, staked it into the ground, and plopped his catch into the water. He surveyed the scene again and decided to try down by the reeds one more time. Coming up empty, he retrieved all of his stuff and walked around the far end of the pond.

He continued on to a small boat dock about half way down the opposite western shore. He fished there for the next hour and a half, catching two more small bass. After eating an apple and two more carrots, he moved a little further down the shore to where a large, flat rock jutted out over the water. He stood on the rock and cast again.

This time, he got snagged on some submerged brush. "Ah, nuts!" he said aloud. He tugged and jerked the pole to the left, to the right, and high over his head. Still, the lure held fast. The lure wouldn't budge. "Come on, come on..."

William pled, as he jerked the line again. This time it gave way and, losing his balance, he tumbled into the pond. Laughter filled the late afternoon air, as he stood up, sputtering, and waded back to shore.

"Silly-Billy! Silly-Billy! Silly-Billy!" Sharon called from the far bank.

Far too irritated for words to express, William clinched his jaw hard, collected his things, and stomped all the way home.

It was a warm afternoon and William had mostly dried out by the time he arrived home. His boots were still a bit sloshy, however. He removed them before going inside, tying them to hang from the clothesline in the back yard. He also removed his socks and pinned them to the clothesline to dry as well.

He then retrieved his fishing gear, lunch bag, and stringer of bass from where he had laid them and entered the house through the utility room door. He decided to store his fishing pole and tackle box in the utility room from then on, and sat them in the corner next to the door. The house was quiet when he entered the kitchen. His mom and dad had not arrived home yet and his grandma had left a note saying she was visiting a neighbor and would be back soon.

After reading his grandmother's note, William set his three small bass in the kitchen sink and put the leftovers from his lunch bag away in the refrigerator. He then returned to the sink and removed the fish from the nylon-twine stringer. Returning this to his tackle box in the utility room, he retrieved his fishing knife.

It took him several attempts to then locate the kitchen cupboard containing the cutting board. He set this down on the counter next to the sink and proceeded to scale and clean the fish. When he'd finished, he placed the fillets in a bowl of saltwater, covered it with plastic wrap, and set it in the refrigerator. He then cleaned up his mess and returned the knife to his tackle box.

By the time he'd had a chance to get to his room and change clothes, his parents were coming in the front door. His father greeted him as he entered the front room. "Hey, there, sport! Did you get out to the pond today?"

"Yep," William replied. "Caught three bass…"

"Were they hogs?" his father asked.

William replied, "Nah, more like fish sticks."

His mother, Theresa, jumped in. "Ah, well…better luck next time, honey. I'll cook them up for you if you'd like."

He replied, "Sure, Mom…they're in a bowl in the refrigerator." He was about to tell them about his grandmother's note when he heard the *rattle-rattle-clank-squeak* of her wagon approaching.

After dinner, William helped do the dishes and took out the trash. Remembering his boots and socks out on the clothesline, he retrieved them before taking a shower and changing into his pajamas. He then read a little from his Bible and took a few practice shots on the pool table out in the game room.

Looking up from the table, he spotted the tall bookshelf, which stood in the far corner. He decided to look for a new book to read. He walked over to the shelf, clicked on a floor lamp which stood nearby, and began to peruse the literary offerings. There were scores of romance novels; all with pretty much western themes. "Yech!" he said. Continuing to browse, he discovered several Bible study books, a dozen or so books on history, a few books of poetry, several cookbooks, a small selection of science fiction novels, and what he assumed must be every *Reader's Digest* since the birth of Christ.

He selected a science fiction novel, turned off the floor lamp, and returned to his room.

The Beast Within...sounds interesting, he thought. He opened his window a bit to let in the evening breeze and turned on the lamp, which stood on the nightstand next to his bed. After scanning the back cover of the book, however, he realized that he was more tired than he had thought. Being out in the sun most of the day had taken a lot out of him. He decided to start reading the book the next day. Clicking off the light, he yawned, stretched, and soon settled into a deep slumber.

Somewhere in the wee hours of the morning, his slumber was disturbed. It was that sound again. Far too faint to awaken him under normal circumstances, the previous evening's encounter subconsciously triggered an exaggerated response. For a few seconds, he was unsure of what had woken him. Then, from the general direction of the kitchen, he heard *scratch, scratch, thump...thump-thump!* When he heard the *snap*! of one of the traps, he sat up with a jerk. "Home run!" he said aloud. He heard a faint squeaking and the sound of the trap being drug around the kitchen floor in a desperate frenzy.

"Woh! Big mouse!" he continued. Curiosity won out over sleepiness and William found himself plodding towards the kitchen. As he drew close to the doorway, the room again grew quiet. He knifed his arm through the doorway, sliding it down the wall. When his fingers located the light switch, he hesitated slightly before flicking it on.

What appeared before William's eyes would haunt his dreams for many nights to come. Against the far wall stood what he assumed must be the famed "kangaroo rat". It was, indeed, the size of a small rabbit. It stood on its hind legs like a kangaroo and had a long, skinny tail with a pronounced tuft of hair on the end. This particular kangaroo rat also currently had a mousetrap securely attached to the end of its tail. This sight was shocking enough, but things then got stranger. As

William's eyes adjusted to the light and he looked closer, he saw something which made him question his hold on reality.

As the hairy creature twitched and dodged to one side, William saw it. Strapped around its midsection, there was what appeared to be… "A saddle?" he finished his thought aloud. He squinted hard and looked again. Sure enough, it looked like a tiny saddle, crafted out of what looked like white leather.

"MOM! MOM! MOM!" he ran screaming from the room. He crossed the main room and ran up the stairs. He missed the doorknob on his parents' bedroom door and crashed straight into the door. The force of the collision knocked him down. As he stood again, the door swung open. A groggy Jacob stood there before him. He scowled at William and asked in a gruff voice, "Hey! Woh! What's up?"

"Dad! Dad! You've gotta' see this!" William replied.

"See what?" Jacob asked in an annoyed tone.

William replied, "Just come! Come! Come! Come!" he continued as he ran back down the stairs.

Unfortunately for William, the kangaroo rat was nowhere to be seen when he and his dad reached the kitchen. Jacob looked around and roughly asked, "What? What, William?"

"But, it was just here!" William protested.

"What was here?" Jacob asked.

"It was…uh…well…" words eluded William. "It was right there!" he concluded, pointing to the trap still lying near the far wall. He walked over and picked up the trap.

"Oh, you caught a mouse…almost," Jacob commented, flatly.

"It wasn't a mouse…exactly," William began. "It was…" he thought of continuing, but became confused and flustered.

"Well, whatever it was, it's gone now. Just quiet down and go back to bed," his father concluded.

William stood there for a moment, confused and frustrated. He gathered his senses somewhat and examined the trap. The spring appeared to be broken. *No, not broken,* he thought. *It's…it's…melted!*

Chapter
Six

William tried to get back to sleep, but found this to be a hopeless task. He tossed and turned for about an hour. Several times, he nearly dozed off, but disturbing thoughts and questions jolted him awake again each time.

Abandoning his hope of sleep, he sat up in his bed, braced his elbows on the windowsill, and stared into the darkness. He found it impossible to sleep with so many unanswered questions flooding his mind. He'd never been able to sleep well when he was aware of any unresolved issue. It was more than just still being upset about the move. It was more than just the damage done to his ego at the pond that day...

Deep inside, what William did not want to admit to himself was that he was afraid. Afraid of what? He did not know... Perhaps that was it; afraid of the unknown. There were so many new things happening in his life... in his mind... in his spirit?

Most of the time, he was uncomfortable... physically. "Growing pains," he'd heard it called. He didn't know how to define it; it was largely an intangible thing. All he knew was that much of the time he had more physical energy than he knew what to do with. And he felt like, well, a snake trying to shed its skin. It just felt like he was squeezed inside too small a package. And most of the time, his body outpaced his brain. He'd become quite accident-prone.

His mind was in turmoil as well. He was having new thoughts and new emotions. He found himself losing interest in what had been some of his favorite pursuits and gaining, well, new interests. At times, William felt as if he were older than his actual twelve years. There were also times when he felt younger. He struggled to understand his identity.

A few weeks before, his father had tried to give him "the talk," but William had blown him off. At the time, he had been just too disturbed and distracted by the upcoming move. *And how can you talk about what you can't put into words, anyway?* he thought.

William was also, for the first time, beginning to have questions about his spiritual life. Up to this point, it was something that he pretty much took for granted. His parents had always taken him to church. It was just normal and he'd never before questioned whether or not he wanted to be there. He'd gone to church camp in the summer and Wednesday night youth group to be with his friends.

But, shouldn't there be more to it? "God has no grandchildren," he'd once heard the pastor say. His parents seemed to have something... something that he knew he hadn't yet laid hold of. William was beginning to realize that there was a difference between knowing about God and *knowing* Him.

With all of this swimming through his mind, William again drifted into that surreal netherworld between waking and sleep. With his eyes mostly closed, his head drifted inexorably towards the windowsill. The side of his head had nearly come to rest on the smooth, cool surface when a brilliant flash of light woke him with a start! Far off to his right, just within his view, there appeared a shaft... a pillar of light. Whiter, purer, and more radiant than lightning; it had appeared for no more than an instant.

Or, had it been an hour? William did not know. It was as if all of time and eternity could have been contained in that one moment. For that moment, or however long it was, time seemed to simply... not be.

And that light! That horrible, wonderful light! It was totally unlike anything William had ever seen. Yet somehow, in some manner he could not comprehend and would have found impossible to describe, it was familiar. A pure radiance... fluid... shimmering and pulsating with... life? It had seemed to erupt from the ground with a benevolent violence, like a power capable of destroying all, yet possessing no desire or intent to do so.

Familiar? Yes, it was somehow familiar. It was as if he were remembering something that he had just seen for the first time. How could something that had appeared for such a brief instant flood his consciousness in such vivid measures? He was both frightened and fascinated. *That was near the blowhole,* he thought.

William spent the following hour or so straining to catch another glimpse of... whatever it had been. He threw open his window and scanned the pre-dawn landscape, leaning as far out as he could without falling into the bushes below. But the world had seemed to return to normalcy. By the time that the golden-orange sun launched its first direct rays over the horizon, William had convinced himself that it had been a dream; a waking dream perhaps, but a dream. *But what about... no, no, just a dream.*

Despite his state of physical and mental exhaustion, William decided to go ahead and get up for the day. *I'll try to take a nap later on,* he thought. He hoped that he could occupy himself sufficiently over the coming hours to crowd the night's strange happenings out of his mind. *Then I can get some rest.* He still hadn't recovered from the four days on the road and being awakened in the middle of the night two nights in a row had only served to amplify his state of fatigue.

William yawned hard, stretching his arms high over his head. He pulled his window closed and latched it. He climbed down off his bed and walked to the bathroom, stumbling over his shoes on the way. He would have fallen, but caught himself on the doorframe leading into the bathroom. Bracing himself, he waggled his head, attempting to wake himself a bit more. This only made him dizzy. "Woh! Not a good idea..."

After nearly falling asleep in the shower, William brushed his teeth and got dressed for the day. He decided to wear the shoes that he's stumbled over instead of his boots, which were still a little damp. Before leaving his bedroom, he retrieved his pocketknife from the top of his dresser. He dropped it into his pocket and headed for the kitchen, eager for breakfast.

As William passed through the main room on his way to the kitchen, he could hear the "tack-tack-tack-tack-ding!" of his mother's typewriter as she worked upstairs. *My, she's got an early start today,* he thought. *I wonder what she's working on?*

William's father and grandmother were standing in the kitchen drinking coffee and talking when he walked in. He wasn't surprised to see his grandmother there, as she was an early riser like him. However, it surprised William to see his dad up. Jacob took a sip of coffee as he turned to William. He swallowed and greeted him. "Hey! Good morning, son!"

"Hey, Pop..." William replied. "What's Mom working on so early?"

"Oh, she's writing some sort of a history article for the state board of tourism, " Jacob began. "I can't believe she landed a job writing for the state, when we don't even officially live here yet!"

"But, why so early?" William asked.

"Beats me," Jacob began. " I guess she's just really jazzed to land her first assignment so soon after moving here. She might end up doing some stuff for the college, too. Speaking of which, " he continued, "I've got to get going." Jacob took one final sip of his coffee, set his cup in the sink, and headed for the front door. "I've got a little paperwork to do at the college today, and was going to go ahead and set up my office... as long as I have to go in anyway." Pointing to a large cardboard box on the dining room table, he asked, "Could you carry that stuff out to the car for me?"

"Yeah, sure..." William replied. He picked up the box and followed Jacob through the front door and out to the car.

"I should be home by late afternoon," Jacob said. "Thanks for your help. I'll bring you a treat from town."

William set the box in the back seat next to a few others and asked, "How about some jerky... the spicy kind?"

"Okay, sure. I'll stop at a gas station on the way back. See you later, son." Jacob opened the front door, slid in behind the steering wheel, and turned the key. As the engine started, he slammed the door, put the car in gear, and began backing up.

William waved as his father pulled away. He took a deep breath, stretched, and soaked in the beautiful morning. Still eager for breakfast, he didn't linger long before he turned around and headed back for the kitchen.

"Scrambled, or over-easy?" Mary asked, as he entered the kitchen again.

"How about an omelet?" William inquired. "I saw a green pepper in the refrigerator last night. Do you have any ham?"

"Sure, boy," Mary replied. "You want some cheese on that?"

"Yeah, thanks Grandma! You're swell!" he concluded.

William poured himself a glass of juice. Collecting a spoon and fork from the dish drainer, he sat down at the small wooden table in front of the window with the blue curtains. As Mary prepared his breakfast, he sipped his juice and paged through a couple of *Reader's Digests* that lay on the table. Feeling a little too warm, he slid the window open a bit. A sudden gust of wind billowed the curtains, catching Mary's attention.

"MMM, smells like rain," she commented as she retrieved three eggs and a gallon of milk from the refrigerator. She cracked the eggs into a glass mixing bowl and added a little milk. She retrieved a wire whisk from a drawer nearby and beat the mixture into a light froth. She then added a little baking soda and beat the eggs a few more strokes. "...makes them fluffier," she explained.

After setting her cutting board flat on the counter next to the sink, she pulled a green pepper, a slice of ham, and a block of cheddar cheese from the refrigerator. She finely diced about a quarter of the green pepper and grated about a cup's worth of cheese. She then diced the ham. With all of her ingredients prepared, she placed a large cast iron griddle on the stove, turning on the two burners that it covered. She proceeded to make William's omelet and a couple of slices of toast for him, as well.

"That fancy enough for you, city boy?" she asked, as she placed the food before him. "You like *Tabasco*, right?" she continued, as she set the small battle of pepper sauce in front of his plate.

"Definitely!" William replied. "Thanks, Grandma." He applied a generous sprinkling of the spicy red condiment to the feast before him and began the happy task of devouring it with gusto.

After William finished eating, he cleared his place at the table, setting his dishes in the kitchen sink. He then collected a couple of empty egg crates from the utility room and headed for the chicken coop. On the way, he stopped at the garden shed. He filled the coffee can kept there with chicken feed and continued on his way. He had now learned to scatter the feed first, before collecting the eggs. This way, the hens would vacate their nests to feed, leaving the eggs readily accessible. He could then easily collect them without getting his hands pecked by the hens.

William walked through the gate and latched it closed behind him. He scattered the chicken feed, doing his best to keep it from falling in front of the door leading into the coop. This way, his path wouldn't be obstructed by feeding hens.

He made his rounds to each nest, completely filling both egg crates, with three extra eggs besides. *Great! How do I get these extras back to the house?* he thought. After a little deliberation, he fit two eggs in his shirt pocket and one in his left front pants pocket. (His knife was in the right pocket.) He left the coop, returned the coffee can to the garden shed, and walked (very carefully) back to the house.

William's grandmother met him as he entered the utility room. "Hey there, boy! ...You fill both those crates?"

"Sure enough," he replied. "...even a few extras." He handed Mary the two full egg crates and carefully removed the extra eggs from his pockets. "See?"

"Quite a haul! Must have been a full moon last night or something," Mary replied.

William had no idea what bearing a full moon could possibly have upon how many eggs the hens laid, but agreed anyway. "Yeah, I guess..."

"Well, it looks to me like we're just about ready to sell some eggs!" Mary continued, as she opened the refrigerator where the eggs were kept. "We've got plenty for now in the kitchen… There's, let's see, eight dozen if we take all but today's two full crates. Why don't we store these and pack the rest out to the wagon?"

She set the eggs in the refrigerator and used the extras William had carried in his pockets to fill in empty spaces in other crates. She and William then carefully placed the other eggs into a cardboard box. "Why don't you carry this out to the wagon," Mary began. It's not that heavy, but if I had one of my fainting spells… let's just say that it'd be harder to sell these eggs already scrambled!"

Most of the time, Mary kept her wagon parked outside the horse barn. William walked out the utility room door carrying the box of eggs and turned left. Mary grabbed her wide-brim hat and followed.

William loaded the eggs onto the wagon, directly behind the seat. He then helped to hitch Chester the horse to the wagon and they were off. They spent the next few hours leisurely traveling to the half dozen or so neighboring homes, which comprised what Mary jokingly referred to as "the suburbs" of Rock Springs. At each stop, Mary waited on the wagon while William made his sales pitch. Of course, being a cordial, small town area, they were always invited in for a visit. This is why it took so long to complete the route.

William didn't mind too much, though. It was his first chance to get to know the area a little. And besides, he managed to sell all eight-dozen eggs. He got quite a few cookies out of the deal, as well.

Another added bonus was that Sharon Stewart hadn't been at home when they came to her house. He did his best to hold back a vengeful grin as her mother apologetically explained that Sharon was at the dentist. William hadn't cared to make public their meeting at the pond, so no one was aware that they had met.

William and his grandmother arrived home just in time for a late lunch. After unhitching Chester from the wagon, Mary turned him loose to graze in the pasture. She and William then returned to the house together.

William wasn't very hungry, as he'd fairly much stuffed himself with cookies on the egg run. He did, however, manage to eat a bowl of soup and most of an egg salad sandwich. As they cleaned up after lunch, he and Mary discussed what he wanted to do with the money he'd collected for the eggs. Pausing in mid-sentence, William heard his dad coming in the front door and bounded out to greet him.

"Hi, Dad! You're back early," he said.

"Hey there, sport!" Jacob replied. "Yeah, it didn't take as long as I thought it would. Is your mother around?"

"She's still typing away upstairs," William replied.

Jacob began walking towards the staircase. He paused and called back to William, "Oh, say, I got your jerky. It's out on the dashboard."

"Did you get the spicy kind?" William pressed.

"Yes, sir!" Jacob replied. This stuff's sprinkled with crushed red peppers. Ought to be a match for your iron stomach."

William felt himself salivating as he made a beeline for the family car. He retrieved the plastic 'jumbo-pack' of jerky from the dashboard and exclaimed, "All right!" He took the pocketknife from his pocket and sliced open the top of the bag. William removed a piece and sunk his canine teeth into it.

"Oh, Dad," William began as Jacob stepped out the front door of the house. "I was going to go check out '*the fort*' today, okay?"

"Sure," Jacob replied. "Just remember what I told you about being careful climbing over loose rocks."

"I kind of wanted to ride my bike out there..." William continued.

"Well, there's a trail that goes most of the way there," Jacob interjected. He pointed out the bare dirt path leading up a distant hill and continued. "There's cactus here and there in the field, so if you don't want to shred your bike tires, stay on the path. You can go on foot when it ends."

Cactus, yeah... I know about cactus! William thought. "Okay, Dad. Thanks."

"Oh, and be sure to be home before dark," Jacob concluded.

William retrieved his bicycle from where he had parked it at the side of the house. He filled his water bottle from a hose-bib and tucked what was left of the jerky into the small cargo pouch hanging underneath the back of the seat. Noticing that the back tire was a little low, he withdrew a compact tire pump from the cargo pouch and inflated it a bit more. He pressed on the tire with his thumb and, satisfied, returned the pump to its place.

He then walked his bike to a gate built into the barbed wire fence, which was close to where the trail leading to 'the fort' began. He made a mental note to remember the location of this gate the next time that he went fishing. He knew that he'd only been lucky when he'd crossed the fence the hard way before. William opened the gate, walked his bicycle through, and latched the gate behind him.

Although there were large rocks scattered here and there, the trail was fairly smooth. It only took William a few minutes to get to the top of the hill. The trail got rougher and a bit windier on the far side of the hill. Being only a recent convert to country life, he was used to flat, smooth, wide streets. He decided to play it safe and walked his bike to the bottom of the hill.

Soon after he reached the bottom, the trail tapered off, so he left his bike and continued on foot. William looked around, attempting to locate the opening to the cave. Here and there, he saw a few old soda cans. Most of these were riddled with small, circular holes. He picked one up and shook it, generating a loud rattling sound. Curious, he turned it upside-down. Several small copper colored spheres tumbled into his cupped hand. *Now I know what I want to save my egg money for!* he thought.

He continued to search for the cave opening. He found a hubcap and an old cap gun, but no cave. He continued searching and stumbled upon a rock lined fire pit. No cave. An arrow lay at the base of the hill. *Cool… but still no cave!* William was beginning to get really frustrated. But just as he stepped around a large clump of brush jutting out from the base of the hill, there it was. In fact, he very nearly fell into it!

Based on his father's description, he had expected to find a great gaping maw; like something you'd build a bridge across. Instead, what he saw was something more akin to a decent sized mud puddle. A hole about six feet wide ran for about fifteen feet along the base of the hill.

"Ah, nuts!" William suddenly realized that he hadn't thought to bring a flashlight. He thought for a moment and decided that there would probably be enough daylight filtering into the cave to at least get a quick look around. He began to pick his way over the large, loose rocks leading down into the earth. After he'd cleared the entrance by several feet he paused, allowing his eyes a chance to adjust to the growing dimness. It seemed to William that the cave went back farther than his dad recalled. But he could see that it tapered off to a crack in the back left corner which was certainly too narrow to squeeze through. He briefly thought of attempting it, but was dissuaded by the horrifying thought of getting stuck somewhere along the way; "swallowed up by the Earth..."

To his right, he could see the old couch his dad had told him about. Poised where he was, he could not believe that they had hauled it all the way out to the cave, and then down over the rocks to the bottom. He guessed that they must have used a flatbed cart or something to haul it from the house to the cave and then were simply stubborn enough to finish the task.

Several folding chairs and a card table stood near the couch. A jar sitting on top of the table caught his attention. He continued down into the cave and walked over to the table. Sealed inside the jar there were several candles and three pocket-sized boxes of wooden matches. *Hey, that'll work!* William thought.

With a little effort, he unscrewed the lid from the jar. He then dumped the contents onto the table. He looked around a bit and found a discarded soda bottle. Using his knife, William shaved one end of a candle until it was small enough to be wedged snugly into the mouth of the soda bottle. He stood his makeshift candelabra on the table and lit it. This task required several attempts due to the age of both the candle and the matches, but was finally accomplished. The dimness of the cave suddenly took on a warmer glow... almost homey in a masculine way.

He then proceeded to look around the cave. It was fairly unspectacular, as far as caves went. William and his family had once toured *Cave of the Winds* while on vacation in Colorado. He'd been awed by the beautiful and intricate formations in the enormous cavern. The tour guide had even pointed out a formation that looked like a king-size slab of bacon.

There were no such formations in '*the fort.*' There were cracks and crevices here and there, but it was mostly just ordinary rock that made up the walls, ceiling, and floor. It was astoundingly ordinary.

Only the mystery of what lay beyond the open crevice in the back corner kept hold of William's pre-teen attention span. He retrieved the candle from the table and walked back to the crevice. He lifted the candle high over his head in an attempt to throw light deeper into the chasm. In the dim and flickering light... it was difficult to be sure... but it looked like it widened out a bit not too far back.

William noted that the closer he held the candle to the crevice, the more it flickered. *A breeze...* he thought. *Airflow; I guess Grandma was right; this must connect to the blowhole somehow.*

He decided to try and make an echo. *If I yell real loud and it echoes,* he thought, *then I'll know that it gets pretty big not too far back.*

He pressed up close to the widest part of the crack and yelled loudly, "Hello!" Quickly, he turned his head so that his ear was right up to the crack. He listened hard. After a few seconds of silence, he heard... something; something very faint. He decided to try again, and yelled even louder, "HELLO!!!" He turned his ear to the crack again. He heard no echo, but... *music?* Like in that place between waking and sleep, he thought, but was not quite sure, that he heard music.

He recalled one of his cousins who lived in Nebraska telling him about 'ghost bells'; how that on very calm days you could sometimes hear the faint sound of bells, like great wind chimes. This despite being miles and miles out in the country and far from any house. His cousin's dad liked to say that, "If you listen hard enough, you can hear the angels..." That was his explanation for this mystery.

But this sound was different. It wasn't like a bell. It was more like... singing. Too faint; too distant to make out any words... it still definitely resembled the sound of a voice. Or many voices, perhaps.

Confused, William stepped back. He looked around and found a fist-sized rock. He tapped on the wall like someone trying to find a good spot to hang a painting. He struck the wall of the cave harder, working his way along the smooth stone surface. Suddenly, at a spot just to the left of the crack, the sound changed. As he repeatedly struck the same general area, he came to an indisputable conclusion. "It's hollow!"

He struck the wall as hard as he could with the rock. It soon became apparent, however, that he would need to bring in heavier artillery. *I can borrow a sledgehammer and come back tomorrow,* he thought. *I think I saw one in the tractor barn.*

Despite his new found excitement, he now realized how tired he was. He decided to take a little nap before heading back to the house. Carefully noting the location of the hollow sounding spot, William returned to the couch. He returned the candle to the table and beat the dust from the couch cushion. Plopping himself onto the couch, he yawned, leaned back, and closed his eyes.

It was a loud peal of thunder that woke William from a sound sleep. "Uh-oh!" he said aloud. He had no idea how long he'd slept, but the candle had burned down to within an inch of the lip of the soda bottle. He left it burning to light his way as he paced across the floor and scampered up the large rocks to the mouth of the cave.

It wasn't totally dark yet. William guessed that it was just after sunset. He climbed up out of the cave and walked hurriedly back to his bicycle. He tipped it up and began walking up the hill. By the time he reached the top, it had begun to sprinkle. Rather than risking a collision with one of the large rocks on the trail, he decided to play it safe and walk his bike back home. It was growing rapidly darker, but the flashes of lightning were frequent enough to provide sufficient light to keep him on the trail.

About halfway home, his dad met him with a flashlight.

"There you are! I was getting a little worried, with this storm coming on."

"Thanks, Dad! I, uh, fell asleep on the couch!" William replied.

Jacob chuckled, "You actually sat down on that ratty old thing?"

"Well, I was really tired," William explained.

"Maybe you should just get to bed a little earlier," Jacob suggested, "even if you are on summer vacation."

"I've been going to bed plenty early, " William began. "I've just been, well, waking up a lot at night."

"That's not too unusual when you're in a new place, " Jacob offered. "Once you settle in a bit more, you'll be fine."

When they arrived back at the house, William parked his bicycle in a sheltered spot under the eaves next to the utility room door. He retrieved the remainder of his jerky from the cargo pouch and went inside. Dinner was waiting for him on the dining room table.

After he ate, William wrote a list of what he wanted to take back to the cave the next day. *Sledgehammer... chisel... flashlight... rope... food...chalk...* He set his list on top of his dresser along with his pocketknife. After a quick shower, he changed into his pajamas. He then sat on his bed and read the first couple of chapters of the book he'd picked out the night before. Feeling very sleepy, he turned out his light, lay down, and closed his eyes. Drifting into an uneasy slumber, he hoped that this night would pass uneventfully.

Chapter Seven

William awoke on Saturday morning to the sounds of thunder and heavy rain. The storm, which had crept in the evening before, had slowly intensified throughout the night. Thick, black clouds now hung low in the sky and a constant re-glazing of rain obscured the view out of his window.

As William braced himself to sit up, he felt the wet blanket. Momentarily confused, he sat up and took note of a small stream of water creeping across the wide windowpane, over the edge, and down the wall to his bed. He had mistakenly left his bedroom window slightly ajar the previous evening.

William grimaced, sighed, and jumped out of bed. A wet bed was not the way that any self-respecting pre-teen wished to begin the day. He pulled his bed out about a foot from the wall, slid behind it, and secured the window. He then felt the blanket again to see just how wet it was. Surmising that it would probably air-dry within a few hours, he pulled it from his bed and spread it out flat on the floor of his room.

He reconsidered and decided to drape it from the edge of the pool table in the game room instead, guessing that it would probably dry faster hanging there than lying flat on the floor. He picked the blanket up and carried it out to the game room. Making sure that only the dry part of the blanket would come into contact with the pool table, he draped the wet side over the edge. Finally, he selected a couple of heavy books from the shelf and weighted the blanket with them to keep it from slipping and falling onto the floor.

William then returned to his room. Noting that the sheets on his bed were only slightly damp, he un-tucked them on the wall side of the bed and allowed them to drape over the edge. "That should do," he said to himself. With this unpleasantness behind him, William walked to the bathroom and got ready for the day. Noting the over-stuffed condition of his laundry bag, he took it with him to drop off in the laundry room as he headed for the kitchen.

As William approached the kitchen, dragging the laundry bag behind him, he noticed his mother at the kitchen sink, washing an apple. "Good morning, Mom," he said as he entered the kitchen.

"Good morning, sweetie!" Theresa replied. "Whatcha' got there?" she asked, looking down at the floor behind him.

"Oh, laundry…" William replied.

Theresa stepped forward, extending one hand. "I'll take that, honey. Thanks." As she spoke, William noticed her gaze shift from him to the dining room behind him. "Oh, my! Looks like I need to dust-mop later on… maybe after I get the laundry started."

William turned around and glanced at the hard wood floor of the dining room. There was a clear, distinct swath of clean floor where he had drug his laundry bag across the room. This extended beyond the dining room and on into the main front room of the house, which also had a wood floor.

Theresa took a bite of her apple as she took the bag from William and carried it to the laundry room. With a fair degree of effort, she swung it high into the air and plopped it on top of the washing machine. She took another bite of her apple and returned to the kitchen.

William was standing at the counter next to the refrigerator, pouring milk on a bowl of cereal. Sliding open a drawer, he retrieved a spoon. He then screwed the cap back onto the milk and turned to the refrigerator, reaching for the handle.

"Oh, leave that out, honey," Theresa interrupted. "I'm going to use it, too."

William set the milk down on the counter and carried his cereal to the small table by the kitchen window with the blue curtains. He sat down and began to eat.

Theresa took a ceramic mug from the cupboard and filled it with coffee. She then poured in a spot of milk and pulled a spoon from the silverware drawer. She spooned in a little bit of sugar and stirred the caramel colored liquid. Taking a sip and finding it to her liking, she removed the spoon and set it in the sink.

"Oh, William," she began, as she opened the refrigerator and removed a flat of eggs, "make sure you stick around after you finish your chores."

"How come?" questioned William, "I was gonna..."

"We're having guests for lunch," Theresa explained, " and Grandma wanted you to help her make some bagels."

"Bagels?" asked William.

"Yep!" Theresa replied. "There's a new recipe she ran across. She wanted you to help her try it out. I'd offer to help her out, but you know me - I burn chocolate milk!" she chuckled.

Feeling a little mischievous, William quipped, "But cooking is women's work!"

As her head whipped around, a crimson flare lit up Theresa's earlobes. This reflex quickly gave way to a knowing grin. "Nice try, mister!" She picked up a spatula and shook it at him. "Finish your breakfast and get to your chores, or I'll show you *women's work*!"

William grinned as he took his last bite of cereal. He mockingly shielded himself with one hand, as he dropped the bowl and spoon into the sink next to his mother. "Don't beat me, Ma'!" he jested. "Ow! Hey!" He skittered away to the utility room as Theresa smacked him on the butt with the flat side of the spatula.

"You'd better wear your rain coat," Theresa called out after him. "It's still coming down pretty heavy out there."

William took full advantage of this opportunity to get in the last word. Just before he let the outside door close behind him, he called back, "Yes, Mother Theresa!"

After William had finished feeding the chickens and collecting the eggs, he returned to the utility room. Carrying the day's collection of eggs, he stored them and performed the egg-rotation before removing his boots and raincoat. He then set his boots in the corner of the room and hung the raincoat up to dry.

Pausing at the kitchen doorway, he was relieved to hear his mother's typewriter pecking away upstairs. His "last word" would hold up, for now. The house was so quiet that he was startled when he entered the kitchen and saw his grandma sitting at the table to his left.

"Good morning, boy!" Mary said. "I didn't mean to scare ya'!"

"Oh, Grandma… I didn't expect to see you there," William began. "I mean, it's just so quiet in here today, and all."

A long peal of thunder rumbled in the distance. "Well, when you've got such a sweet song going on out there, there's no sense in drowning it out with a bunch of noise," Mary replied. There was another rumbling of thunder as a sudden gust of wind ruffled the blue curtains. "Yep, despite man's best efforts, God still makes the sweetest music." From somewhere in the distance, a hawk's shrill cry echoed across the pasture.

Several seconds of soft melody passed before the spell was broken. "Well, anyway… you ready to bake, boy?" Mary asked. I've already got all the stuff laid out on the counter over there." She motioned to the far counter, to the right of the kitchen sink.

"Sure, Grandma," William replied. "What kind of bagels are we making?"

"Oh, it's kind of a Mediterranean recipe," she answered. It's got sun dried tomatoes and basil and stuff like that. It sounded like it would go really well with the soup I'm serving for lunch."

As they walked to the counter together, William asked, "What do you want me to do?"

Mary answered, "Well, I've already mixed the dry ingredients; flour, salt, sun-dried tomatoes, basil, oregano… could you mix the yeast?"

"Uh, ok…" William hesitantly replied.

"It's the stuff in that paper packet there," she explained. Just mix it with about a cup of lukewarm water…. *lukewarm…* not hot!"

William filled a measuring cup with lukewarm water from the sink. He then picked up the packet of dry yeast and tore open one end. He dumped the contents into the water and stirred it gently with a spoon.

"Now, add a little bit of sugar, " Mary instructed. William added about a teaspoon of sugar and stirred once more. "That's fine, boy. Just set it aside for a bit." William pushed the mixture to the back of the counter.

"Do you know how to separate eggs?" Mary asked.

"Um…" William joked, "tell nasty rumors about the other egg?"

Mary laughed so hard that she got light-headed. "Oh, don't do that to your poor old granny!" she said, as she caught her breath. She then proceeded to demonstrate the technique for separating eggs for William. He caught on quickly, and did the others she had laid out. Mary explained, "We're going to use the whites, mixed with a little milk, to glaze the bagels before we broil them."

"Broil?" William asked. "I thought you baked them?"

"Well, actually… you bake them *first*, then *boil* them, then *broil* them to finish them off," Mary explained, as she added milk, water, and the yeast mixture to the dry ingredients. She pinched and mashed and folded all of the ingredients together with her strong hands in order to form a sticky dough. It was a little too wet, so she added a handful of flour. She mixed and folded the dough in on itself again until it pulled away freely from the side of the mixing bowl.

"You have to cook them *three* times?" William asked, wide-eyed.

Mary spread a thin coating of flour on the countertop as she explained. "Well, you just bake them until they're about half done. Then you boil them; that's what makes them chewy. Then, you glaze the tops with the egg whites and broil them to finish them off." She pulled the dough from the bowl and set it on the flour-covered portion of the counter. After kneading it several times, she returned it to the bowl, which she then covered with a towel. "Now we've got to let it rise for awhile, " she concluded.

"Are they gonna' be ready for lunch?" William inquired.

"Sure, no problem," Mary assured him. "I'll turn the stove on to pre-heat in a little bit here. When we start to bake them, I'll turn the water on to boil and while they are boiling, I'll switch the oven to 'broil'… it's all in the organization, boy!"

"How long do they have to rise?" William asked.

"Oh, about an hour… maybe a bit longer," Mary replied, thoughtfully. "I'll call you when it's time to form the bagels."

"Ok, thanks. I think I'll go do something in the game room," William concluded. "Maybe I'll check out that big toy box in the corner..."

"Oh, my… yes!" Mary interrupted, "You should enjoy that. It's full up with toys your daddy and his brothers and sisters played with when they were young."

"Really, wow!" William inquired, wide-eyed once again.

"Yep," Mary continued, " I had them all stored away until a few weeks ago. I decided to bring them out and put them in that old trunk for you. You should really enjoy looking through all those old treasures. They really made some quality stuff back then... not like the mindless junk they turn out nowadays."

William walked back to the game room and pulled the large black trunk away from the wall. He uncoupled the latch and lifted the lid. "Wow, cool!" he repeated over and over, as he sorted through the childhood dreams of another era.

After a little better than an hour had passed, Mary poked her head into the game room. "You ready to make bagels?" she asked.

William returned the miscellaneous toys to the toy box, closed the lid, and followed her out to the kitchen. She showed him how to form the bagels. "You just pinch off a glob about this big," she began. "Then roll it out like this... that's right. Now," she continued, "pinch the ends together to make a bagel. Good! Now, put it on the cookie sheet there. No, not that close... spread 'em out a little... that's better."

Do we stick them in the oven now?" William asked.

"Not quite," Mary replied. "We've got to let them rise again; for another half-hour or so. We can clean up this mess while we're waiting."

They cleaned up the kitchen as they waited for the bagels to rise again. Mary then slid them into the oven and turned the water on to boil. When the bagels were done baking, she dropped a few of them at a time into the boiling water to cook for a minute or two. She and William then placed the bagels onto the cookie sheets again, patted them dry with paper towels, and brushed on the egg-white glaze. A couple of minutes under the broiler for each sheet of bagels finished off the process.

"Man, that's a lot of work for a bagel!" William declared, as he removed the last batch from the broiler to cool.

"Well, I can tell that they are going to be worth it," Mary replied, as she sniffed the delicious aroma.

"What kind of soup are we going to have with these?" William asked.

"Oh, it's kind of a minestrone," Mary replied. I added some diced garlic and used lamb instead of beef... changed around a couple of other things, too. If you want a taste, it's keeping warm in the crock pot over there..."

Just then, Theresa entered the room. "Oh, my goodness!" she said. "It smells terrific in here!"

"Thanks, dear," Mary replied. The boy here was quite a help. I think he kind of enjoyed it, too."

"Yeah, kinda'," William admitted. "Where's Dad today?" he asked.

Theresa replied, "Oh, he's off reading somewhere. In this big of a house, it's hard to keep track of him. With this delicious smell wafting through the house, though, I'm sure he'll be showing up soon."

Moments later, the doorbell rang. Theresa began to head for the front door, but paused as she heard Jacob bounding down the stairs. "Goodness! ... Sounds like a herd of elephants falling down the stairs!" She shook her head and continued on to the front door.

Mary turned to William as she opened a cupboard door. "If you could take these out to the table for me," she began, "I'll get the table set while you go out and join your folks. There's somebody out there that I'm sure you'd like to meet." She winked at William as he took a stack of plates and bowls from her hands.

Uncomfortable with the obviously veiled meaning of the wink, William walked out to the dining room and set the pile of dishes on the table. He then hesitantly continued on to the front room.

"There's our boy," Jacob said, as William entered the room.

There on the couch, in front of the fireplace, William saw a man about his dad's age, with blondish-brown hair and a slender mustache. Seated next to him was a tall, slender woman with auburn hair. William remembered her from... from his first egg delivery. "*Oh, no...*" he thought. "*No, please...*"

"William, I'd like you to meet Mr. and Mrs. Stewart," Jacob continued. "They live just down the road."

"Oh, yes! We've met," Mrs. Stewart recalled. " Say, we'll be ready for more eggs in a day or two..." She addressed William directly now.

"Ok, sure..." William said, as he nervously glanced around the large, open room. "Say, is..." he began, weakly.

He was interrupted by Mr. Stewart. "Shari, come out here, please."

In short order, Sharon Stewart emerged from the game room. Her face was covered with a knowing grin, which betrayed the fact that she held leverage over William's head. "Hi, Billy!" she snipped.

Mr. Stewart paused slightly. "Oh, have you two met?" he asked.

Oh, yeah... we've met!" Sharon replied. The tone in her voice and the gleam in her eyes threatened to tell the whole story of their prior encounter. "How's your, uh..."

"Fine! Just fine!" William coldly bit off the words as he glared hard at her. He almost wished that he had a rock in hand... or within reach.

"Well, that's nice!" Mrs. Stewart chimed in. Apparently, the adults were unaware of the pre-pubescent tension permeating the room. "Why don't you two run along and play until lunch is ready?"

"But, uh..." William began, "I've gotta' help Grandma... set the table! Yeah, that's it!"

"That's alright, I'll help her finish up, sweetie," Theresa interjected. " Why don't you two go play pool or something for a few minutes?"

William began to protest again, but knew that it would be fruitless. He sighed, and relented. "Fine..." He set his jaw and marched stiffly to the game room, with Sharon skipping along lightly behind him. The blanket from William's bed still hung from the pool table. He casually felt the hanging edge... it was almost completely dry.

"The game's *eight-ball*," William declared, as he removed the blanket from the table and tossed it into his room. He set aside the books he'd used to hold the blanket in place, and then gathered the balls, assembling them neatly in the triangular rack at the head of the table. "...You know how to play?" he asked.

"Sure do," Sharon replied, "I play with my dad sometimes."

William removed the rack and consented to letting her break. He assumed that she wasn't very good; after all, she was a girl! If nothing went down on the break, the balls would be scattered, and he would have the advantage.

CRACK!... thump, thump-thump, thump...

William scowled as two balls, both of them *stripes,* went in on the break. He thought for a moment that he would get lucky, as the cue ball rolled directly towards a corner pocket. *...scratch on the break, automatic loss!* This flicker of hope dissipated however, as the cue ball stopped just short of the pocket. A measure of satisfaction returned as Sharon missed her next shot.

A small triumph... the corners of William's mouth curved upward slightly. He circled the table as Sharon stepped back. Taking just a little too long to pick out an obvious shot, he finally pointed with the end of his stick and declared, "...seven in the side." The maroon sphere obediently dropped into the side pocket, leaving the cue ball set up for a cross-corner shot on the three. William called his second shot and made that one, as well.

He was feeling pretty confident now. He called a long rail shot on the six ball for his third attempt. This was the most difficult kind of shot for him, but he was fairly confident that he could make this one. The cue ball was just far enough away from the rail to give him a little bit of angle. *"Just don't hit it too hard,"* he thought. *"...Hit it too hard, and it'll come off the rail."* He took a deep breath, letting it out slowly as he placed his front hand. He eyed the dark green six ball, trying to gauge just exactly where to make the cue ball strike it, so that it would slide smoothly along the rail to the corner pocket at the other end of the table. Confident that he had sighted the magic spot, he tested the slide of his stick, paused slightly, and took one smooth stroke at the cue ball.

Unconsciously, he attempted to influence the ball's path with his body language, much as a bowler does. "Come on, come on, come on..." he pled, under his breath. It was a beautiful shot - almost. The six ball rolled straight and true down the near rail, heading directly for the corner pocket. He hadn't put quite enough on it, however, and it came to rest about a quarter of an inch from dropping in.

"No, no…" he moaned.

"You got robbed!" Sharon grinned. "Nine - eleven combo in the corner," she pertly declared. She'd obviously been pondering the shot while William played. She quickly lined the shot up and cleared the eleven ball from the table. She missed her next shot, however, and it was William's turn again.

"Six in the corner!" William confidently proclaimed as he stepped forward. He lined up the shot and easily made it. "Four in the side…" He made that shot, as well. The next shot was a little more difficult; another long rail shot. William tried his best to find a different shot but, not knowing how to jump the cue ball, this was the only one open to him. He called it and then spent a good thirty seconds studying the shot. He took a deep breath, held it, and rammed the cue ball! To his great relief, he made it. "Yes! Yes! Yes!" He danced with glee.

"Silly-Billy…" Sharon muttered softly.

William ignored her and lined up his next shot. He now had only two balls left to make, plus the eight.

"Hey, William!" Theresa called. "Didn't you hear me?" (He hadn't.) "It's lunch time; wash up!"

William was caught off guard. "No, but Mom, I…"

"Now, young man!" Theresa cut short his begging.

"But, " he pled, "but I've only got…"

"Come on, Sharon," Theresa cut him short again, "I'll show you where you can wash up."

Sharon threw a spiteful grin in William's direction and replied, "Yes, ma'am."

William's bubble was burst. It was no use trying the shot now. Even if he made it, Sharon wouldn't believe him. "Dang it!" he muttered under his breath. He dropped his stick onto the table and walked into the bathroom to wash his hands.

During lunch, Mr. and Mrs. Stewart commented on how good the food was. "Thank you so much!" Mary replied. "William here made the bagels."

"Really?" Mrs. Stewart asked.

"Well, I helped, anyway…" William sheepishly replied.

Mrs. Stewart leaned in towards her daughter and feigned a whisper. "…handsome *and* he can cook!" Sharon grinned at William and mockingly winked. William's face blushed redder than his mother's hair.

When everyone was done eating, William helped his grandma clear the table. He was about to slink away to his room when his dad intercepted him. "Hey, sport! Your mom and I are going to play cards with the Stewarts for awhile. Why don't you and Sharon go play outside? The rain's stopped and it seems to be clearing up. Why don't you show her around the ranch?"

William was about to protest when Sharon interjected. "Wanna' go fishing?" she asked, slyly. William glared at her, coldly.

"Hey, why don't you show her the fort?" Jacob asked. "I bet she'd like to see that."

"What's '*the fort*'? " Sharon asked.

William cut off his father's response. "Oh, I would, Dad, but it's kinda' far for her to walk…"

"Oh, that's ok, I rode my bike over," Sharon said.

"*Great, now I'm trapped!*" William thought. "Well, ok then…fine…"

William was very disappointed. He'd wanted to take a hammer and chisel back to the cave and see if he could break through to the hollow spot he'd discovered. There was no way that he was about to let Sharon Stewart in on that cool of a secret, though. He decided that he would pack his stuff up that evening and leave early the next day. *"If I don't let her in on the crack or the hollow spot,"* he thought, *"hopefully she'll get bored quickly and won't want to go back there again. Maybe I could even pretend to not be able to find it..."* He then realized that wouldn't work. *"Nah, Dad knows I've been back there already..."*

"Come on," he said, "my bike's out back."

Sharon replied, "Mine is in front. I'll meet you out back in a minute." She slipped through the front door as William headed towards the back door, via the kitchen. He walked through the utility room and opened the door leading outside, after pausing to put on his shoes. The rain had stopped and there was a hint of a rainbow high in the sky. He shut the door behind him and walked over to his bicycle. Just then, Sharon rounded the corner of the house and peddled up beside him. She stopped and got off her bicycle.

"So, which way do we go?" she asked.

William nodded towards the distant hill and began walking. Sharon followed. "It's on the other side of that," he said. "We should walk the bikes until we get across the fence."

"How do we get through the fence?" She asked.

"There's a gate a-ways down there," William replied. He paused and then snidely asked, "Are you sure that *girly* bike of yours can make it?"

"Look, boy!" she began, "I've ridden this bike on rougher ground than you've got here. I'm more worried about your scrawny little chicken-legs making it!"

"Yeah, whatever!" was the best comeback William could muster.

"Silly-Billy," Sharon retorted.

They walked in silence the rest of the way to the gate. William opened the gate and latched it again after they both had passed through. The path leading to the distant hill was only wide enough for one bike, so Sharon followed him back. The recent rainfall made the trek a little slower than the first time William had gone to the fort, as mud caked on their tires.

When they reached the top of the hill, William slowed down and stepped off his bike. Sharon followed suit. "It's a little steep on the way down... and with the rain and all," he began.

"Yeah, ok..." she agreed.

They left their bikes on top of the hill and walked down the far side. William looked around a bit when they reached the bottom. Something was different, but he couldn't tell what. *"It's just the rain, I guess..."* he thought.

When they reached the large bush that obscured the cave entrance, William stuck his arm out. "Careful," he warned, "It's just around here." He stepped carefully around the bush and stopped at the edge of the chasm.

"Cool!" Sharon said. "How big is it?"

Wanting to tame her enthusiasm, William replied, "Oh, it's just a little thing... ready to head back?"

"No way! I want to have a look around!" she replied. Sharon began to work her way through the mouth and down into the cave.

William hit his head on the way in, but squinted hard and kept himself from crying out. He bit his lip and rubbed his head until the pain passed. Several feet into the cave, they both paused while their eyes adjusted to the dimness. They then continued down into the cave, until they reached the floor.

William nonchalantly pointed out the couch and card table. Noticing the candles, Sharon picked one up. She retrieved a match from the jar on the table and used it to light the candle. She held the candle high in the air with one hand and casually looked around for a few minutes. William was encouraged that she seemed to be getting bored quickly. "Cool," she said, rather flatly. "Well, I guess we'd better be getting back..."

"YES!" William thought.

Sharon blew out the candle and set it back on the table. Together, she and William returned to the house. William parked his bike and went to his room to do some reading, while Sharon paged through some magazines in the front room.

After about half an hour, the Stewarts left for home. William found his list of supplies for exploring the cave the next day and collected them before dinner. He stuffed everything into a small backpack and set it on top of his dresser.

They had a chicken and rice dish for dinner that night, along with broiled tomatoes, topped with grated cheese. William wasn't used to this fancy cooking yet, and ate more than he could ever remember eating before. "Looks like you're beginning to grow into your daddy's appetite," Mary commented.

After helping with the dinner clean up, William played a couple of solo games of pool. He then read another chapter of The *Beast Within* before changing for bed. It was a clear, starry night with a cool breeze, so he opened his window a crack before retrieving his blanket and making his bed. He then pushed the bed back into place against the wall and crawled under the top cover. Although he was an early riser by nature, he wanted to be sure to be up early for his caving expedition the next day, so he set the alarm on his clock. He then grew still and faded off to sleep.

Chapter
Eight

William awoke a little earlier than usual the next day. At first, he was unsure that he *was* awake... He'd slept so deeply that he felt almost numb as he opened his eyes. The air was permeated by an unearthly stillness and a faint amber glow painted a stripe on the far wall of his room. William couldn't remember ever sleeping this deeply before and it kind of scared him. He felt as if he'd literally sunk down into the mattress; and must now forcibly un-fuse his flesh from the fabric.

Suddenly, he felt it. As he yawned and began to sit up, an enormous stretch took possession of his body. William was thrown back onto his bed, as he whined in ecstasy. Every muscle and tendon, every bone and sinew seemed to be doing its best to pull him apart into a dozen pieces. Just as he neared the breaking point of physical tolerance, the assault relented. *Oh, that feels good!* he thought.

William was wide-awake now. He inhaled deeply, filling every cubic inch of lung capacity, and then letting out the breath in a staccato puff. He sat up, facing the far wall of his room. The amber glow had now faded to a somber shade of orange. Something undefined, which had lodged itself in the deep recesses of his mind, was being triggered by the radiance before him.

A puzzled look covered his face, as he cocked his head to one side, staring down at the floor. Faint, vague images randomly leapt into and out of his conscious mind. It was like being absolutely certain that you knew someone's name, yet not being able to recall it; like grasping at a reflection.

Then, suddenly, he remembered the dreams... strange dreams, vivid dreams of pure, raw elements. The fire, the water, the piercing, brilliant light... dreams of stone and flame and torrential rain and... and incomprehensible beauty!

There were memories, memories of things undefined and unknown to the modern world of man, yet somehow familiar. A terrible chill of revelation pulsated within William. The music! The singing he'd heard (or, had he?) that first day in the cave... he had heard it again in his dreams. There was something ancient about it, something holy. The music; the sound itself seemed *alive*. Something about it made William feel... small. He squinted his eyes hard and clenched his fists as the flood of sounds and images threatened to overload his mind. He felt as if he were being swallowed up by something larger than himself.

Finally, mercifully, the flood of revelation subsided and William returned to the world of plastic, concrete, and aluminum. Some bizarre, obnoxious clatter had shaken him, wrenching him from his otherworldly interlude. He inhaled sharply as the wondrous splendor around him faded to the more familiar surroundings of his room. Turning to his right, he shut off the alarm clock.

He then stood and stretched again. Choosing to ignore the strange brush with another realm, he turned to gaze out of his bedroom window. The sky was aglow with hues of molten glass. A single, brilliant shaft of sunlight stood like a fiery pillar on the far horizon. Obviously, the sun was nearly up. The beam of sunlight reminded William of the radiant shaft he'd seen in the field two nights previous. He still hadn't gone out to see the blowhole, but was now more determined than ever to do so.

William stretched again, and then straightened the covers on his bed before walking into the bathroom. He removed his pajamas, stuffing them into his laundry bag. He then brushed his teeth and splashed some cold water onto his face. He looked into the mirror above the sink and raked a black comb through his dark, wavy hair before returning to his bedroom.

A basket full of clean, folded laundry sat on the floor at the foot of his bed. He carried the basket to the far side of his room and set it on top of his dresser before selecting a pair of jeans, a t-shirt, and a pair of socks. He would put the rest of his laundry away later.

After getting dressed, William grabbed his backpack of cave exploring supplies and started out to the utility room. As he passed through the front room of the house, he heard a thunderous roar coming from upstairs. *Goodness, Dad!* he thought, *You snore like a grizzly bear!*

He continued on through the dining room and into the kitchen, where he left his backpack sitting on the small table by the window with the blue curtains. Pulling his boots on in the utility room, he grabbed a couple of empty egg crates and started across the back lawn. On his way to the chicken coop, he glanced again in the direction of the blowhole. William noticed that the area immediately around the location of the blowhole, where he'd seen the strange light, looked somehow different from the rest of the pasture. *Weird,* he thought. *It's, well, greener than the rest of the pasture… and, well, something else…* He finally decided that perhaps it just looked different because of the big tree next to it, or that maybe the shade from the tree kept the ground from drying out as fast as the rest of the pasture, which had full-sun most of the day. *Or,* he thought, *of course!! The cows like to hang out there... fertilizer!* Something told William that this explanation wasn't quite up to par, but he figured that it would do for the time being.

He continued across the back yard to the garden shed at the far end, where he retrieved the day's allotment of chicken feed. He then fed the chickens and collected the eggs. As he exited the coop on his way back to the utility room, he noted numerous strange footprints in the dust around the outside of the coop. *Those almost look like hands,* he thought. *I wonder if those are from raccoons?* He decided to ask his grandmother about it later on.

He returned to the house and, after storing the eggs, walked into the kitchen to eat a quick breakfast. He opened the refrigerator and, surveying the shelves, selected a leftover slice of apple pie. He poured a glass of milk for himself, retrieved a fork from the silverware drawer, and took a seat at the table by the window.

As he began to eat, William could hear the raucous noise of snoring reaching a new crescendo upstairs. He was dumbfounded that he could hear it all the way in the kitchen. *Mom must be climbing the walls!* he thought.

William finished eating and, as he set his plate, fork, and glass in the sink, noticed the coffee pot on the counter. It was still half full from the day before. He pondered this new venture for a moment before retrieving a small saucepan from the cupboard and filling it with the leftover coffee. He placed the pan on the stove and turned it on to medium. He kept a vigil on the dark liquid, until it began to steam. He then turned the stove off and pulled a large mug from the back of the counter, filling it to the brim with the reheated coffee. It quite nearly overflowed, but he stopped it just in time.

William had tried coffee once before, but didn't really like it. However, his dad called it "wake up juice". He was beginning to feel a little sleepy again and wanted to be wide-awake for his caving expedition. *Maybe if I add a little sugar,* he thought.

He sipped enough coffee from the cup to make enough room for sugar, and then spooned in a generous helping. Stirring the sugar in, he took another sip. "MMM, that's better," he commented.

He took his seat again, sipping the hot, sweet liquid. Noticing that the snoring upstairs had stopped, he thought, *Gee, I hope Mom didn't smother him!* His grandma's Bible sat at the back of the table, with her picture of Seth, William's grandpa, sticking out of one edge. As William continued sipping the coffee, he opened the Bible and studied the photograph. *I really miss him,* he thought. When he finished emptying the mug, he returned the aged photograph to its place of honor. He then walked over to the sink and placed the empty mug alongside the other dishes, before retrieving his backpack from the table. He lifted the heavy bag and strapped it on, preparing to leave.

Just as William stepped through the utility room doorway, a voice called out from behind him. "Hey, where are you off to, boy?" Mary asked.

William stumbled, nearly falling, as he spun around while still in forward motion. "Oh, hi Grandma. I'm heading back out to the fort today. I thought I'd poke around a little more."

"Sorry, boy… not today!" Mary replied. William's jaw dropped slightly, as a look of confusion spread across his face. "Don't you know what today is?" she asked.

"It's, um…" William began, "it's…" He thought hard, but could not grasp what his grandmother was getting at. *"Golly, I hope that the Stewarts aren't coming over again,"* he thought. *"At least not if 'Shari-Pie' is with them…"*

"It's Sunday, silly boy!" Mary interrupted. "You'd better take off those old rags and pick out some nice church clothes. Your mom and dad will be down for breakfast in a little bit."

William was devastated! Not wanting to show the depth of his disappointment, however, he set his backpack down just inside the utility room door and flatly replied, "I ate already." He then removed his boots, setting them next to the backpack.

"Really?" Mary inquired. "That's too bad, you're gonna' miss out on my biscuits and gravy."

William's salivary glands sprang suddenly to life. "Well, maybe I could eat one... or two..."

"Or, twelve?" Mary completed his thought.

William grinned, "Well, maybe..." Still disappointed at having to wait another day for his caving expedition, he glanced back towards his backpack and sighed before returning to his bedroom to change clothes.

Pulling the door closed behind him, he paced over to his closet. He removed a pair of black slacks from a cubbyhole on the left, tossing them onto his bed. He then slid several hangers to one side, finally selecting a light blue dress shirt with pinstripes. Although he despised them, he knew that his mother would insist on him wearing a tie, so he selected one of the several clip-on ties she'd bought for him. He then returned to his bed. Removing his clothes, he tossed them onto the floor by his nightstand. He then changed into the shirt and slacks he'd selected and put on his best pair of black shoes; what he referred to as his *dress-sneakers*. Finally, he clipped on the tie. He walked into the bathroom and retrieved a comb to tuck into his pocket before walking out to the game room.

He racked the balls on the pool table and took a dozen or so practice shots, before returning to the dining room. His mom and dad were just sitting down as he entered the room. As he took his seat, Mary entered from the kitchen, carrying a bottle of *Tabasco* and a large wicker basket full of biscuits. She set the biscuits and pepper sauce on the table and began to return to the kitchen to retrieve the gravy. Jacob jumped up from his seat, interrupting her. "Hey Mom, let me get that; it's probably a little heavy."

"Oh thanks, son," she replied. "Just keep your thumbs out of the bowl!" Mary took her seat and muttered, "...Never could keep his thumbs out of the gravy," as Jacob strolled towards the kitchen.

Several seconds later Jacob returned, carrying a large country-blue bowl of sausage gravy. He carefully set it in the middle of the table next to the biscuits and returned to his chair, licking his right thumb clean as he took his seat. Mary raised an eyebrow and nodded at Theresa, who grinned as she snickered in agreement.

William managed to eat two biscuits before offering to help clear the table. "Thanks, dear," Mary replied. "Just set the dishes in the sink to soak. I'll take care of them this evening."

"This *evening*?" William asked. "Where are we going to church, Denver?" He hoped that it wasn't one of those 'full-gospel' places, where they give you THE *FULL* GOSPEL, all in one sitting.

Theresa replied, "No, Silly-Billy," (William cringed) "we're going to your grandma's new church in Phoenix, and then out to lunch afterwards. And then maybe we'll spend a little time at the mall."

"Grandma's church, in *Phoenix*?" William asked, as he turned to Mary. "You haven't been driving that old wagon all the way to Phoenix, have you?"

"The Sanders down the road took me in each week," she replied. "Real nice folks, they drove me to the doctor in Phoenix whenever I needed it, too."

William turned back to Jacob. "Dad, if we're going to the mall, can I bring my egg money?" He thought of the b.b. gun he wanted to buy, but didn't think that he had enough money saved yet. Still, if they were going to a mall, he wanted to have some money on hand.

"Sure, sport," Jacob replied. "You've worked hard for it, you can decide how you'd like to spend it." After a brief revelatory pause, he concluded, "Within certain limits, of course!"

William finished setting the breakfast dishes in the kitchen sink. He then filled the sink with hot water and squeezed in a little dish soap. Before joining the others in the family car, he returned to his room and retrieved his egg money, which he kept in one of the pockets of his *Charlie Davis* curtains.

William yawned loudly as he took his place in the back seat of the car and pulled the door shut. "What's the matter, sport?" Jacob inquired, "...still not sleeping well?"

"I don't know how anybody in Arizona could have slept last night," William replied, as the car began to move.

Theresa interjected, "Why's that, honey?"

William quipped, "Dad snored like a dying grizzly!"

Jacob exploded in laughter, nearly veering off the road! Theresa fell silent, flushing red, her eyes burning holes through the windshield. Mary tried not to grin, as she muttered "Oh, my!" under her breath.

"What? What?" William asked.

"Um, that wasn't *me*, son..." Jacob replied.

"Huh? Well... who then?" William began. "Oh! No..."

"That's right boy, it was *Momma-Bear!*" Jacob replied. Theresa smacked his leg hard as he chuckled.

William was terribly confused now, not knowing how someone so small could snore so big. However, he figured that if he wanted to make it to his twelfth birthday, he'd better drop the subject. He sat back and looked out the side window, feigning interest in the scenery.

A few moments later, they reached the grand old weeping willow tree where their road intersected with Interstate 17. Jacob slowed the car and turned left, heading south towards Phoenix. About twenty-five minutes of Sunday morning scenery passed before they exited the highway again, turning right. A few more minutes of travel brought them to a small side street, where they turned again and pulled up to a large stucco building with a tall tower of sorts in front, topped by a cross. The building was tan, with a large sign to the right of the door, which read, *Paradise Valley Community Church.*

As Jacob entered the parking lot and turned off the engine, Mary turned to William and said, "I started to come here a few months ago. I think you're really going to like this church."

"I miss my old church..." William replied flatly.

As they all stepped out of the car and began walking, Jacob interjected, "I checked this place out when I was down here interviewing at the college. They've got a lot of really neat youth activities; I'm sure you're going to like it. It'll be a great place for you to make a bunch of new friends."

Yeah, whatever... William thought. *Maybe I can get a decent nap out of it, anyway.*

"What's the pastor's name?" Theresa asked.

"Um, I don't know," Jacob began. "They were interviewing for a new pastor when I was here."

Theresa turned to Mary with the same question in her eyes as they reached the front door. Mary just grinned and walked into the church, with the rest of the family following.

Several feet inside the door, Mary extended her hand to a tall, lightly bearded man with chestnut hair. "Good morning, Reverend!" she greeted the man.

"Why! Good morning, Mary!" the man replied. "Awfully good to see you! Did your son and his family make the trip out here alright?"

Jacob stepped up beside Mary as she said, "Yes, sir! This here's my baby boy."

Jacob rolled his eyes slightly as he extended his hand. "Good morning, I'm Jacob Thornton," he said.

The tall, bearded man took Jacob's hand, shaking it vigorously. "Glad to meet ya'! I'm Reverend Jim Jones." Jacob's grip slackened. The pastor leaned in towards Jacob and, through grinning lips, assured him, "No relation..." Jacob glared at Mary, his face betraying a trace of chagrin.

William was really caught off guard by the music playing as they entered the sanctuary. He was expecting some dried up old lady sitting at a dusty piano. And maybe some skinny old guy with his pants hiked up to his chin, playing an accordion. But what he saw and heard was something entirely different.

The main sanctuary was a huge open room with high ceilings. Towering triangular windows near the top of the walls let in a lot of natural light. They were tinted a light shade of purple, filling the room with a peculiar radiance. At the far end of the room, there was a large, slightly elevated stage. There was no dusty old piano or toothless old man with an accordion, however. Instead, there was a dark haired man of perhaps thirty years of age with an electric guitar. To his left stood a slightly shorter woman with long, blonde hair. She was singing and playing an acoustic guitar in front of a microphone. To the man's right stood a trumpet player, a woman playing a flute, and a saxophonist. Near the back of the stage stood a bass guitarist and next to him, a drummer playing a drum set-up of perhaps twenty different pieces.

William was once again thoroughly confused. This did not look or *sound* like church as he knew it. The music sounded like... "Jazz?" he asked aloud. "In church?" He stared blankly at his grandmother.

That's right," Mary replied. "They also play rock and roll, and even a little reggae sometimes."

William thought that she must be joking, until he noticed a set of steel drums standing in the back corner of the stage. He stared blankly at Mary again.

"They also do hymns sometimes; but probably not like you're used to hearing them," she continued. "Aw, come on boy! Just because I'm a grandma doesn't mean that I don't like to cut loose and boogie!" William dropped his head and slipped into a row of seats near the back. Jacob, Theresa, and Mary slid in next to him. "Pastor Jones figures that there's gonna' be all kinds of people in Heaven, so why not get used to all kinds of music in church now?" Mary concluded. "There's quite a bit in the Psalms about praising the Lord with stringed instruments and loud, clanging cymbals... sounds like electric guitars and drums to me!"

To his surprise, William found himself actually enjoying the service. That was, until the sermon began. The pastor spoke on *bitterness and resentment*. William came under the assault of conscience and made the deliberate choice to ignore most of what was said.

After the service had concluded, William and his family had lunch at the *Big Boy* drive-in down the road from the church. They then drove to a large mall on the outskirts of Phoenix. William went to check out the toy and hobby stores as Mary and Theresa browsed the bookstores. Jacob said that he wanted to check out the sporting goods store. Before they dispersed, they all agreed to meet at the main entrance in three hour's time.

William rode the escalator to the second floor and bought an *Orange Julius* at the food court on his way to a large toy store his grandmother had told him about. There was a *NO FOOD OR DRINK* sign at the entrance to the store, so he had to stand outside window-shopping until he'd finished his drink. He then threw away the empty cup and began strolling the aisles. Not much caught his fancy, although he found the model rocket kits somewhat interesting.

After about forty-five minutes, he decided to look around some other stores. He bought a soft pretzel and another *Orange Julius* before taking the escalator back to the first floor. He looked at the guitars in a music store for awhile, before spotting the sporting goods store at the far end of the mall. *Maybe I'll check out the b.b. guns,* he thought, *just for fun.*

William began walking towards the sporting goods store, waving to his mom in the bookstore as he passed. She was just inside the door, flipping through a romance novel called *On Winds of Change.* He briefly caught sight of his grandmother farther back in the store, looking at the magazine rack.

When he arrived at the *Sportsman's Paradise* store at the far end of the mall, he scanned the numerous aisles. "Wow! That's big!" he said aloud. Just about thirty feet down one of the aisles, he spotted a store employee restocking a display. "Excuse me, can you tell me where the b.b. guns are?" he asked.

The woman looked at him suspiciously for a moment, and then replied, "...back left corner."

"Thanks," William said, as he continued down the aisle. He continued on through the aisles, weaving his way around other shoppers, until he reached the back of the store. As soon as he turned to the left, he stumbled upon the object of his quest. *Wow, there must be thirty different kinds!* he thought. He walked along, checking out each different model as he went. Some had adjustable sights, some had real wooden stocks, while others came with stand-up targets that you cut out of the back of the box. *350 fps, 270fps, 575fps…* William didn't know what *fps* meant, but he guessed that the bigger the number, the better it was.

"How's it going, boy?" Mary called out from behind him.

"Oh, hi Grandma. Okay, I guess," he replied. Just then, he spotted a bright yellow sign that read *CLEARANCE.* He scanned down the shelf until he saw an orange tag with the price. *Hey! I've almost got enough for that,* he thought. *Maybe I could borrow a little…* "Grandma," he began, "could I borrow a couple of dollars until we do another egg run?"

"Oh, you don't want to spend your money on that," Mary replied.

"But, I really want to get a b.b. gun!" William said. "And this one's on clearance. Please, I'll pay you back in a couple of days!"

Mary leaned in towards William. "Let me rephrase that," she said. "You don't *need* to spend *your* money on that!" She winked at him and twitched her head in the direction of Jacob, who was obviously pretending to look at basketballs a few aisles away.

Yes! William thought. *All right!* "Thanks, Grandma," he whispered. I think I'll, you know, go look somewhere else." He walked back to the bookstore, where he looked around for awhile before buying a book on cave exploration. He flipped through it as he sat on a bench near the main entrance, waiting for his parents.

That night, William tucked the book into his backpack before changing for bed. After brushing his teeth, he read another chapter of *The Beast Within* before setting his alarm clock and turning off his light. At first, he was too excited to sleep; both because he now knew that he was getting a b.b. gun for his birthday and because he was finally going to get the chance to return to the cave and investigate the strange hollow spot he'd discovered. As the night grew dark and cool, however, he was lulled to sleep by the songs of an owl and the distant rumbling of thunder.

Chapter
Nine

William slid in behind the steering wheel and pulled the door closed. It was a warm day, so he rolled the window down. He then adjusted the mirrors and stuck the key into the car's ignition. As he turned the key, he pumped the gas pedal vigorously. The car sprang to life with a deafening growl, which soon settled to more of a fine-tuned purr.

He let the engine warm up for a minute or two before switching his foot to the brake pedal. He held the brake pedal down firmly, as he first released the parking brake and then shifted the transmission into drive. Slowly letting off the brake, he shifted his foot over to the gas pedal again and began slowly accelerating down the dusty country lane.

The day was dry and hot. Clouds of dust boiled up into the morning air behind him as he sped along. He didn't know exactly where he was going, but *he* was the one driving; that was all that mattered. Wherever this dusty, bumpy country road led him, *he* was in charge of getting there. He had *control*. It was all up to him.

William comforted himself with this thought as he continued driving. The scenery, which had at first been comforting and familiar, was beginning to change. Before long, he no longer recognized anything about his surroundings. Had he taken a wrong turn somewhere? He did not know. In addition to not knowing where he was going, he now had no idea where he *was*. Although this confused him, he was not really frightened. He was still the one driving. He was still the one in control. That was *all* that mattered. That would do.

As William continued driving towards his unknown destination, something was suddenly different. He wasn't sure *what* at first, but something felt... different. Without warning, the car lurched hard to the right, turning onto a broad side road, which led down a steep hill.

A sudden flush of panic overtook William, as he slammed hard on the brake pedal. Nothing happened! He let off and tried again, pumping the brakes repeatedly. The car did not slow down at all. Grasping the steering wheel with an iron grip, he tried to turn the car. The speeding automobile paid no heed to his demands, but seemed to have come alive with a will of its own.

It was about then that William realized that he was dreaming. But if he was dreaming, how could he know that, consciously? How could he, while asleep, be aware of that fact... consciously? This was truly a strange experience, one that was totally new to William. But he knew it to be fact.

However, knowing that fact did not alleviate his growing concern over his present dream-state crisis. He grasp the steering wheel even harder, while nearly pushing the brake pedal through the floorboard. With all of his strength he turned the wheel, which finally yielded to his demands. *Yes!* he thought, *Now I'll finally break free.*

But this was not to be. Although the steering wheel did turn and yes, the tires began to give way, the direction of the car's travel did not change! Instead, it began to spin in a counter-clockwise motion, with the brakes fully locked. There was a terrible grinding sound as the spinning automobile continued its descent down the long, steep hill.

It must be more than simple gravity taking it there, William now knew. There must be some unseen force at work; one far greater than Earth's allotment of gravity could muster. As he fearfully struggled to regain control of his destiny, the car continued its unyielding journey into the unknown, drawn by some celestial force with the consumptive resolve of a black hole. William fought with every ounce of determination he possessed, but it was clear that his strength was both inadequate for and inconsequential to the present crisis.

Just as the car reached the bottom of the hill, the consuming force seemed to slacken. The car slowed, straightened out, and came to a stop. William, shaking somewhat, hung his head in relief and took a moment to compose himself. He then raised his head again, gazing through the dust-covered windshield.

There was something out there in the distance; something… beautiful. He did not yet know what it was, but it intrigued him. Some distance away, far across the barren landscape, just where the sky met the earth, there seemed to be an oasis of sorts. Hues of emerald and aquamarine graced the far horizon.

His curiosity hopelessly aroused, William opened the door and stepped out of the car. Instantly, his perspective shifted and he *saw himself* from some distance to the left of the car where he was standing. *Wow, this is strange!* he thought. He was conscious of being next to the car, but also of seeing himself from some distance away… both at the same time.

As William continued gazing at the distant lake (he now knew that's what it was) he felt a deep yearning for it. He was hot and dusty and thought that a swim in a nice, cool lake would be wonderful. Besides, it was so beautiful; so captivating.

However, he had become aware that he… that is to say, his dream-self… did not know how to swim. He was profoundly disappointed. Despite the allure of the beauty before him, he was resigned to remain where he was; barren, dry, and joyless.

Then, the strange got stranger. He heard a sound behind him and caught just a glimpse of the back door of the car opening. *What?* he questioned. *I was in that car alone. There wasn't anyone with me!* He saw feet step out of the car and the bottom edge of a white robe.

A shadow then fell across the ground next to his dream-self. Somehow, the shadow betrayed the identity of its owner. As his dream-self spun around, his face flushed white and his eyes grew wide. But William could see only the face of his dream-self, not the One approaching him.

William's view shifted again. He now seemed to be seeing through the eyes of the One who'd been in the back seat of the car; who had now picked up his dream-self, cradling him in His arms.

The unseen figure now began carrying William towards the distant lake. He walked along slowly, but His intent was somehow evident. He was carrying William to the lake.

William again realized that, in his dream, he did not know how to swim. As they drew closer to the lake, William grew increasingly uneasy. Before long, the unseen figure stood right at the water's edge, with William still cradled in His arms. The water was incredibly beautiful, but he was overwhelmed with fear. He had lost control of the car; his ability to control his own destiny. And now, he found himself carried by a will greater than his own to the brink of something that, although enticing, frightened him terribly.

William sensed a deep and abiding compassion radiating from the figure holding him. He wanted to trust, but somehow thought, *You just don't understand! I can't!*

In the wink of an eye, William found himself airborne. The mysterious figure had thrown him out over the lake! He arced high into the air, then began plummeting towards the water below! As he inhaled sharply, paralyzed with fear, he saw the hands that had cradled him extend towards him.

The hands... powerful hands, yet exceedingly gentle... hands calloused by hard labor... and scarred by iron spikes. From these hands which had crafted the hydrogen atom, and from that humble beginning flooded the entire cosmos with life-giving radiance; from these hands which first formed man from the dust of the ground, and then drew a companion from his side... from the hands which fashioned the tree that was used to extinguish His life... the hands which had carried William to this place... from these hands now blazed an awesome grace! A brilliance unmatched erupted from the outstretched hands, enveloping William; suspending him in mid-air over the lake.

That light! He'd seen it before! It was the same blazing, fluid brilliance that had flashed in the field that night; yet now in even larger measure somehow. Was this being, this One who had carried him here, the ultimate source of this living light? Was he *the* source... the source of *ALL?*

Chapter
Ten

William awoke with a start! Shaken and confused, he shot up and spun around in a daze. Locating the source of the zealous clamor that had awakened him, he gradually came to his senses. Reaching over to the nightstand, he shut off the mettlesome alarm clock. His heart racing, he surveyed the room.

For a moment, his mind was a void. Then, the memory of the dream suddenly invaded his consciousness. The intensely vivid imagery overwhelmed him briefly and he had to brace himself against the nightstand. He'd had vivid dreams before, but this was the first time he had ever felt awake -consciously aware- *inside* the dream. The duplicity of the experience both startled and fascinated him. The strange mixture of conflicting emotions and impulses was something akin to what tornado chasers must experience. William pondered the bizarre vision as he paced to the bathroom and began to prepare for the day.

Inexplicably, he knew that there was something different about *this* dream; that this dream was something more... *more than just a dream.* It was more than just random thoughts or unconscious emotions ricocheting around behind his eyeballs as he slept. William somehow knew that this dream... this dream had another source; a source outside of himself.

And it had meaning. He knew that this dream had meaning... and purpose. It was a vessel of revelation. Driving the car meant control; having control of his own life, his own decisions, his own future. The road he traveled was dry and dusty and the landscape, barren. Still, what had been important to William was that he was the one driving, the one in control.

Then, he had suddenly lost that control. Or, had he never *really* had it? Whichever the case, William had found himself no longer in control of his own fate. He careened into the unknown, fighting it every inch of the way, overcome with fear.

Then, when the terrifying descent down the hill had come to a merciful end, he became aware of something new, something beautiful in the distance. He deeply yearned for... whatever it was. Yet, he was afraid of it at the same time. Whatever *it* was, he knew that it was beyond him, beyond his ability to receive and to experience. He felt as if the beautiful thing in the distance would certainly overwhelm and destroy him, at least in his present state. Yet, he also somehow knew that whatever it was, was necessary; vital to his existence. And yet, fear... and shame... kept him from it. He did not have the courage or resolve within himself to journey across the desolate landscape in pursuit of that beautiful oasis beyond.

It was at this point that he had become aware of a presence; a presence both benevolent and terrifyingly resolute. In this presence, William had sensed both a fiery compassion and an unyielding determination that would not yield to his insecurity and would not be swayed by his fear. Although he could sense compassion in this presence unlike any he had ever known, William had still become filled with terror as this presence began carrying him towards the lake. He was truly divided within himself. Yes, he knew that he could (or at least *should*) trust the One carrying him. But if this One really did love him, how could He be carrying him towards something that filled him with such fear?

"*It is **because** I love you,*" a voice from within him seemed to say. "*Holiness is more important than happiness.*"

This thought leapt suddenly into William's mind, catching him off guard in the middle of brushing his teeth. He froze in mid-stroke, with the toothbrush sticking out of the side of his mouth. He attempted to wrap his mind around this profound thought, while staring down at the bathroom sink. He did begin to understand the concept, but only a mite. William knew that there was a much bigger revelation contained in these words than he could understand at that time. But a tiny spark had now ignited within him. With time, that spark would grow. Over the coming months and years and decades, this spark would birth a flame. And that flame would become an all-consuming fire.

The sensation of toothpaste-laden drool streaming across his cheek shook William from his torpor. He finished brushing his teeth and laid the toothbrush aside, before splashing cold water on his face. He then quickly dressed and made his way to the utility room.

Strapping on his boots, William slipped out the back door and across the yard. Making short work of feeding the chickens, he collected the eggs before returning to the kitchen. He decided on a stack of oatmeal-raisin cookies and a glass of milk for breakfast. *Oatmeal **and** fruit,* he thought. *That's breakfast food.*

As he finished off the last of his milk, William glanced down at his grandma's Bible, which lay open on the table. Highlighted in orange, he read:

"Trust in the Lord with all your heart,
and lean not on your own understanding;
In all your ways, acknowledge Him,
and He shall direct your paths."
* Proverbs 3:5-6 (NKJV)

William drained the last drop of milk and set the empty glass in the sink. Just then, his dad entered the kitchen to refill his coffee cup. "Good morning, son," Jacob began. "What's my boy up to today?"

"Oh, hi Dad," William replied. "I'm, um, heading back out to the cave. I'll probably be gone most of the day."

"Are you planning on making it back for lunch?" Jacob asked.

William replied, "Nah, I've got some snacks and stuff in my backpack. I'll be fine."

"Are you taking some extra water along?" Jacob inquired. "It's supposed to get pretty hot today."

"Um, Oh yeah! I saw a canteen hanging in the utility room," William replied. "I'll fill that up and take it along."

"Okay, sport... have fun," Jacob said. "I'll see you at dinner."

William paced to the utility room and found the old canteen. He carried it to the mop sink and filled it with cold water. As he turned to retrieve his backpack, Jacob called out, "Oh, don't forget... I want to take you fishing down on the river sometime this week!"

William glanced back and nodded in agreement as he stepped through the back door. Glancing over at his bicycle, his face suddenly fell. The back tire was flat. Upon closer examination, he could see a length of heavy bailing wire protruding from it. "Ah, man!" he exclaimed.

"What's wrong, boy?" Mary asked, as she rounded the corner of the house. Glancing down at the tire, she concluded, "Oh, flat tire, eh?"

William scowled, "I was gonna' head back out to the cave today. But I don't want to walk all that way with this..." He dropped the backpack and canteen next to his disabled bicycle.

"Well honey, your mom's heading in to town later on," Mary replied. "I'll see if she can pick you up a spare tube and a patch kit. You do have a tire pump, don't you?" she asked. "If not, I'll have her..."

"Yeah, but what about today?" William interrupted. "I really wanted to get back out to the cave *today!*"

Mary thought for a moment and then suggested, "Well, why don't you take Chester? I taught you how to ride last summer, didn't I?"

"Chester?" William hesitantly replied. "Um, I don't know..."

"Aw, come on... you did great on him last summer," Mary encouraged. "It's in your blood, boy. And you know Chester's a good horse. He won't stampede on ya'. Just be sure to tie him up, so he don't walk home on you while you're pokin' around in the cave."

With a long walk carrying the heavy backpack and canteen as his only alternative, William finally relinquished his objections. "Well, okay... I guess," he sighed. "Will you help me get him ready?"

"Sure, follow me," Mary replied. She whistled to Chester, who was plodding across the middle of the pasture. The horse's ears perked up and he obediently trotted over to Mary, who opened the gate to let him through. She then closed the gate and took hold of Chester's bridle, leading him to the horse barn. William retrieved his backpack and canteen and followed behind. He had a little trouble keeping up with the brisk pace and reached the barn a couple of dozen paces after they had arrived.

Following Mary's instruction, William saddled Chester and clipped a set of reigns to the horse's bridle. Mary double-checked the saddle straps. "Very good, boy," she said. "You learn quickly. Now, you be sure and let him get a good drink before you head out. It's gonna be a hot one today. And try to tie him up in some shade, if you can," she concluded. "I think there's still a couple of big trees not too far from the fort."

"Okay Grandma, thanks!" William said, as he placed his left foot in the stirrup and swung up onto Chester's back. He steadied himself and took hold of the reigns. Mary handed him his backpack and he strapped it on. She then hung the old canteen from the saddle horn, triple wrapping the strap so that it wouldn't swing around too much. "You remember how to steer this animal?" she asked.

"Yeah, it's coming back to me," William replied. "Thanks again, Grandma. I'll be home around dinner time."

On her way back to the house, Mary opened the gate in the fence again, allowing the horse and his somewhat hesitant rider to pass through. William then allowed the horse to drink his fill of water from the trough just inside the fence before they set off across the pasture. Wanting to finally get a look at the blowhole on his way back to the cave, William steered Chester in that direction.

When they arrived, William did not find what he had expected. There was no trace of… *fertilizer* in the immediate area around the blowhole. All that he saw was a nearly perfect circle of very lush grass, about ten feet across, dotted with wildflowers. And in the middle, nearly hidden by the foliage, a circular hole about eight inches in diameter. It would have been a dangerous pitfall, but for the constant breeze rising from it, which made it difficult to miss. Even from his perch atop Chester, William could feel the cool air wafting up from the depths. There was a hint of sweetness in the air, which William assumed must be from the wildflowers.

I can see why the cows like this spot, he thought. *But I don't understand why... how come it's so green here, just in this spot?* He thought for a moment, then finally decided that there must be an underground spring seeping up to the surface in that spot. *I'll bet it seeps up through cracks around the blowhole.* He thought back to something he'd read in the book about caves he'd bought at the mall and concluded, *Yeah, that must be it.*

William carefully stepped down off of Chester and located a rock about the size of a golf ball. Poised above the dark void, he held the stone captive. Cocking his ear to one side, he loosed his grip and began counting, "one, Mississippi... two, Mississippi...three, Miss -" He was disappointed when he heard the stone strike bottom in a little less than three seconds. He was hoping that it was deeper than that.

His curiosity satiated, William climbed back aboard Chester and prompted him in the direction of the cave. With the exception of the area around the blowhole, the pasture was already beginning to dry out for the Summer and Chester kicked up a good deal of dust as he walked along. Soon, the man who leased the pasture from Mary would have to start running the irrigation lines which were stacked up next to the pond.

William was eager to explore the cave and was beginning to become impatient with the horse's leisurely pace. However, the memory of his recent experience with the cactus was still quite fresh in his mind. He dreaded the thought of falling from the horse and landing on cactus again. Thus, he decided to play it safe and allow the horse to continue lazily sauntering along.

Before long, they had made their way to the spot where the trail began to ascend the distant hill. Chester continued at a steady pace as the trail wound its way up the hill and down the other side. As soon as they reached level ground, William dismounted. After a stretch and a yawn, he led Chester to a shady spot under a large oak tree some distance past where the eastern slope of the hill trailed off to level ground again.

William then took a lead rope from the saddlebag. After clipping one end to the horse's bridle, he tied it off to a low branch of the oak tree. Retrieving the canteen, he poured a little water into a cupped hand and rubbed it onto Chester's nose to help him cool off. The horse snorted in appreciation.

Next, he adjusted the straps of his backpack, and then hung the canteen from his shoulder as he stepped off in the direction of the cave. He covered the distance in just a few moments' time. Pausing slightly at the cave's mouth, he adjusted the backpack again before beginning his descent. The sun had climbed well into the morning sky and a good deal of light spilled down over the rough slope and across the floor of the cave. He did not need to pause to allow his eyes to adjust this time. However, he did pause for a moment when he reached the bottom of the slope, in order to reacquaint himself with his surroundings.

He then paced over to the far left corner of the cave, setting his backpack and canteen next to the large crack in the wall. He scanned the wall for a moment before opening the top of his backpack. Rummaging through the contents, William retrieved the hammer and a stick of white chalk. He began tapping on the wall in front of him with the hammer, attempting to determine where it would break through with the least amount of effort.

As he tapped on the wall with the heavy hammer, he listened carefully and made marks with the chalk where it sounded the most hollow. When he was confident that he had fairly accurately defined the area where he would concentrate his efforts, William stepped back and returned the chalk to his backpack. He had defined an area, roughly oval, about three feet across at its widest point. *It's a little high*, he thought. *I don't want rocks falling on my head... I need something to stand on.*

He set the hammer down and glanced around the cave, spotting the dusty couch first. There was also an old wooden crate, which seemed to serve as an end table of sorts. Off to the side a bit stood the card table and several folding chairs. He paced over to the subterranean living room in order to more closely examine his prospects.

The crate looked far too fragile to hold his weight. One of the chairs *might* hold him; but then again, it might not. It could suddenly collapse on him, or he might simply lose his balance and fall. Obviously, the rickety old card table wasn't even a consideration. "I guess it's the couch," he said aloud. With a great deal of effort, he walked the old couch across the cave floor. He alternately lifted the opposing ends of the couch into the air, swinging them this way or that, until he had successfully transported the dusty old beast into proper alignment with the back wall of the cave. Sipping a little water from his canteen, William took a moment to catch his breath before continuing.

He then retrieved the hammer and a heavy chisel from his backpack. He balanced himself on the front edge of the couch and went to work. The stone was somewhat softer than he thought that it would be, and he had soon circumscribed the area defined by the chalk marks. He made his way around the oval several more times, deepening the chiseled groove a little more with each orbit.

Finally, William felt as if he must be nearly through. He tossed the chisel off to the side. Making sure of his balance, he grasped the hammer with both hands. With all of the force his nearly twelve-year-old frame could muster, he raised the hammer high over his head and brought it crashing down on the stone wall in front of him.

The outcome of this action was not exactly what he had hoped for, as the stone refused to give way. Instead, the force of the recoil sent William tumbling over the back of the couch! Having been lucky to avoid any serious injury, he retrieved the hammer from where it had flown and returned to his perch. *I'm glad Sharon wasn't here to see that,* he thought as he braced one hand against the cave wall. *Okay... plan- B!*

Instead of trying to break his way through with one mighty blow, he now steadied himself with one hand, while swinging the hammer with the other. At first, there was no visual indication that his efforts were doing any good. However, he somehow sensed that he was making progress.

After several strokes, the sound of the hammer falling against the stone seemed to change somehow. Soon after, two large cracks appeared. A few more strokes sent smaller cracks fleeing in all directions. Finally, the stone gave way and a small hole appeared near the middle of his designated passageway. Energized by this small success, William made short work of completing his oval portal to the underworld.

He stepped down and returned the hammer and chisel to his backpack. He then retrieved his flashlight and stepped back onto the couch. Grasping the flashlight in his right hand, he turned it on; its beam invading the mysterious beyond. He extended the flashlight through the opening and peered in.

What he saw was another room, roughly the size of the one he was in. But the hole he peered through was only about a foot below the level of the ceiling in this next cavern. The floor was a dozen feet or more below him and appeared to slope quite steeply downhill as it neared the back wall. A few rocks and small boulders were scattered here and there.

As the hungry beam consumed the darkness, William suddenly heard a scampering sound off to his right. He quickly flashed the beam in that direction and caught a glimpse of movement! He scanned the ceiling, the walls, the floor… just as the beam bathed a particular boulder in white light, he saw movement again. Something had ducked behind that large rock!

Too excited to be afraid, William jumped down off the couch. He quickly retrieved his backpack and canteen. After pulling a length of rope from the backpack, he tied it off to one of the couch's heavy wooden legs. He then tied the other end of the rope to the canteen strap and slowly lowered it through the hole and to the floor of the cave below. Zipping the backpack closed, he dropped it through the hole as well.

William then inserted the flashlight into one of his pockets and mentally prepared for the task ahead. Bracing both hands on the edge of the portal, he swung one leg up and through the opening. *Just like getting on a horse,* he thought. Firmly gripping the rope, he swung his other leg through the hole and began lowering himself to the cave floor below.

As soon as his feet were steady on the cave floor, William quickly pulled the flashlight from his pocket and ignited the beam once again. He caught his bearings and flashed the beam in the direction of the large rock where he'd seen the movement. Slowly he crept forward, until he was within about eight feet. He then pivoted around the stone in one quick motion, igniting the back side. *Nothing!* Whatever it had been was no longer there. *Nuts!*

Slowly surveying the rest of the cave, William strained at the silence. In the middle of the left wall, a crack opened. He assumed that it must be a continuation of the crevice in the room above, where he'd thought that he heard music. As he looked closer, there appeared to be a series of regular, flat shapes sloping uphill, hidden within the crevice. The shapes were very regular and very even; *like a… a staircase?* William thought. *Now, that's weird!*

He swung the beam back to the opposite wall. In the far corner, there appeared to be an opening; a passageway leading farther back into the earth. He lifted the flashlight over his head, vainly attempting to see farther down this new passageway. But his current position would not allow this. He decided to walk over and check out this passageway first, to see how far back it looked like it went. If it looked interesting enough to warrant investigating in depth, he would return for his backpack; or at least for a piece of chalk to mark his way so he didn't get lost.

As William began to carefully pick his way across the steep slope leading towards the back wall of the cave, he suddenly heard the scampering sound again. It was coming from behind him now! He hesitated slightly, before spinning around, launching the beam in the direction of the sound. What he saw… he could not believe! There, frozen in the flashlight's beam, was the strangest and most frightening thing he had ever seen!

About six feet behind him, atop a large stone, stood a kangaroo rat about the same size as the one he'd seen in the kitchen. That was not the strange part, however. A creature of that size could easily scamper through the crevice on the far wall and it would not be unusual for them to use underground places of this sort as nest sites. But this particular rodent was also wearing a saddle! It looked nearly identical to the one the kangaroo rat in the kitchen had worn. And beside the saddled rodent stood… William did not know what it was!

Next to the kangaroo rat, holding a tiny set of reigns and obviously paralyzed with fear, stood what vaguely looked like a little person. He, or *it*, was humanoid in form, but quite different in appearance. Roughly eight inches tall, it stood upright, with arms and legs that were somewhat spider-like; very slender and slightly longer in proportion to its body than a human's. The creature was wearing clothing of a sorts, but what skin William could see appeared to be a light shade of gray. A neat tuft of white hair crowned the creature's head and its eyes looked somewhat oversized.

As William took one very hesitant step in the creature's direction, the mutual spell was suddenly broken. The gray creature deftly leapt aboard the kangaroo rat, which sprung into motion like an auburn bolt of lightning! It was obviously making a beeline for the crevice on the left-hand wall. Abandoning all sense of caution, William sped off across the floor in pursuit of the tiny rider. He just barely managed to cut in front of the kangaroo rat, blocking the creature's escape.

In one smooth motion, the rodent and his rider wheeled around and sped off towards the opening in the opposite wall. William chased after them again and might have caught up. However, about halfway across the cavern, the rat suddenly stopped and spun around. The tiny creature on its back raised a hand into the air.

There in the depths of the earth, in a place of darkness, there suddenly exploded a fiery brilliance! A luminosity unmatched by a thousand suns instantly blinded William and he felt as if his whole being were dissolving; being infused into something far beyond himself. *That light! That horrible... wonderful light!*

Every muscle in his body went limp in that instant. And yet, the inertia of his pursuit carried William forward. He fell, striking the floor with a horrendous force. As the dreadful light had blinded his eyes, now breaking bones and tearing flesh laid siege to his mind. As William tumbled down the steep slope, blinded with pain, his head finally struck the back wall of the cave.

Then all was black.

Two Men

Two men,
living in one skin,
battling for control…
One must die,
the other shall fly
to the champion of his soul.
To realms of light
in star-blazed flight
to dance before the throne;
precious gems
we are to Him,
who kneel to Him alone.

But first the flame,
first the fight,
first the pain,
and first the night...
First the race,
and then the prize.
First the dust,
and then the skies.

Until that day,
we yet remain
battling the darkness,
overcoming the pain…
Two men,
living in one skin,
battling for control.

Michael M. Middleton
from Sacred Journeys
copyright 2002

Chapter
Eleven

Vaguely, William realized that he must be dreaming again. Having been knocked unconscious, his mind was somewhat blurred, but he gradually became aware once again of that bizarre sense of being awake inside of a dream. In some minute measure, he was aware of the events of the day which had brought him to this point. However, his mind was currently focused on the reality he now found himself immersed in.

At first, he simply *felt*. He had no sense of vision or sound, nor any sense of these being absent. He did not feel as if he were blind or deaf, but the only sense he noticed at first was a sensation… a feeling of floating, of being suspended; of being *in-between*.

He also experienced a strange sensation of decompression. He felt as if he were… expanding. It was as if he, his very being, had been compressed inside of a vessel of some sort and was now being released.

As his essence escaped its earthly shackles, William felt himself being drawn upwards. (He had no idea how he knew that this was 'up', but that's what it felt like.) This was by no effort of his own, but through some immutable natural law. As a cork released from one's grasp at the bottom of a swimming pool needs exercise no effort in order to rise to the surface, so he, having been released from that which bound him to the dust, simply rose.

In an instant of graceful repose, William suddenly felt himself coming to rest. He had arrived... somewhere. In a carefully synchronized flood of revelation, he gradually became aware of the sensation of vision. Initially, it was simply as if he were encompassed by a thick fog, intermingled with its substance. As his being congealed, he became aware of being surrounded by the mist, but no longer a part of it. All was a hazy, brilliant white. How big was this place William now found himself? He did not know. He had no sense of *big* or *small*, but only of limitlessness.

Before long, the haze began to clear a bit. In front of him, William now saw something truly awesome in the distance. From out of the mist, there suddenly appeared a great hall of white stone, veined with silver. Grand columns rose skyward to his left and right and at the far end lay an enormous slab of white stone. *An altar,* he somehow knew.

This altar rose from a seven layered foundation, forming a staircase which surrounded it on all sides. Although there was a truly awesome radiance encompassing everything in all directions, what William saw in the very center of this display put even that to shame. Rising from the very center of the altar was a brilliance that could not be believed if it were not seen. A pillar of pure, liquid, living light erupted with a glory beyond comprehension. This fluid, radiant brilliance surged and pulsated with an inexhaustible, self-sustaining potency that truly made William feel... small.

Despite the ferocity of the power before him, William was not afraid of it. Or, at least part of him was not. He was suddenly overcome once again by that otherworldly sense of duplicity; of being in two places at once. Of being two people at once.

He felt a sudden sense of weight in his arms. Glancing down, he found himself to be carrying... himself. Or rather, a copy of himself; like an identical twin. However, there was something different about this twin. Radiating from this other self, William could see and feel darkness. This other self seemed to be a repository of sorts. Sharply etched on its face was everything negative within William; all the fear, anger, and bitterness... all selfishness and pain and greed and envy. Within this *other* there seemed to reside all of William which was dark; everything which was not pure. This creature embodied everything that was unlike the brilliance before him.

Instinctively, William knew the task that was being asked of him. The impurity, the filth, the *self* which he carried; all things of the lower nature must be sacrificed upon that altar. All impure motivations, all fear, all greed, all envy, all that was of darkness must be exposed to that light, there to be consumed.

There was no one forcing him to this task; no booming voice from the sky or spear to his back. There was no act of bribery or coercion coaxing him to do what he knew he must. He simply knew that he must, of his own free will, choose.

And yet, how can one of his own free will choose to be put to death? William's identity was so intertwined with that which he was being asked to sacrifice, that he could not understand how he could sever himself from it. Though he did not understand how, he knew that in order to live, he must allow a certain portion of his being to die.

The struggle he now undertook threatened to strip William of his sanity. He felt himself -his consciousness, his will- torn wildly back and forth between his two natures. Just as he believed that he had summoned sufficient courage to approach the altar with his despicable cargo, that lower nature would launch into a vicious assault. Fear, anger, and self-justification would attack him in dynamic waves.

Following a monumental struggle, light and truth finally won the battle. But only by the narrowest of margins. With conviction burning through every fiber of his being, William fought his way to the gleaming altar of stone. At the very moment he set his lower nature upon the altar, the nature of the fiery pillar of light somehow changed.

The blazing, pure white radiance remained totally undiminished. But now there was something more. It was as if what he had sacrificed had functioned as a prism of sorts. Swimming within the pillar of white radiance, there now appeared blazing orbs of color. Spheres of molten emerald and ruby... topaz and sapphire... citrine and beryl... rose from the dissolving form before him and majestically spiraled upwards as a fit offering.

William had won a mighty victory. But he somehow knew that it was only a beginning. There would be many more battles. There would be many more struggles in the sacrifice of self. And yet, this was a beginning. Bathed in this knowledge, the scene before William began to fade.

"...If anyone desires to come after Me, let him deny himself, and take up his cross, and follow Me. For whoever desires to save his life will lose it, and whoever loses his life for My sake will find it." Matthew 16:24-25 NKJV

Chapter
Twelve

The glory before William gradually blurred and faded to blackness. As his awareness once again invaded the world of dust and thorns, the first sensation he became aware of was that of cold stone against his cheek. The coolness was pleasant, but then came the pain. A dull ache saturated every cubic inch between his temples and flashes of fiery alarm radiated from torn flesh and broken bone elsewhere.

As he became fully awake once again, the pain overwhelmed him. He would have cried out, but a crushing pain in his lower back prevented it. He could only breathe in shallow, staccato gasps.

At first, the pain so overwhelmed him that he did not recall the strange creature he'd been chasing after when he fell. As he caught his breath, however, the memory returned. Fear now became the companion of pain. How long had he been unconscious? He did not know. What kind of a weapon had blinded him, causing his fall? Was that bizarre creature, whatever it was, even now lurking in the shadows… waiting to finish him off?

The shadows! The realization suddenly struck him. There were shadows on the wall if front of him, including his own. That meant that his flashlight must still be on, and laying somewhere behind him. He began to sit up, pushing against the stone floor with his right hand. A sudden intensification of pain and a distinct weakness told him that this was not a good idea. He collapsed again onto the cave floor.

William now braced his left hand against the stone floor and awkwardly pushed himself up to a sitting position. Cradling his right arm, he examined it in the dim light. It was slightly swollen from his elbow down and bent where it shouldn't. It looked like there was an extra joint midway between his elbow and wrist.

Realizing that his arm was broken, a sudden wave of fear overtook William. He knew that there was no way that he would be able to climb up the rope to get out of the cave with a broken arm. If his dad did come looking for him in the fort, would he notice the passageway leading to this previously unknown section of cave? Would he be able to yell loudly enough to get his dad's attention?

William's thought shifted to the task of taking stock of his other injuries. A fiery pain throbbed in both kneecaps, but he did not think that either one of them was broken. His left ankle was badly sprained and he did not know if he would be able to walk. Besides that, he had a number of cuts, abrasions, and deep bruises on his arms and legs and an egg sized lump on the back of his head. He carefully dabbed his left hand on it and then examined his fingers in the light. *No blood... that's good.*

As William drew a deep, painful breath, he suddenly froze. A new wave of fear flashed up his spine! The shadows on the wall in front of him... they were moving! He was obviously not alone. Not knowing what to do... not knowing what he *could* do, he was paralyzed for a minute or more. Finally, he slowly shifted his weight and turned to face the unknown.

There, silhouetted by his flashlight's fading amber glow, stood a hundred or more tiny gray creatures like the one he'd chased after. Forgetting his injuries, William attempted to stand and flee. The ensuing explosion of pain reminded him, and he crumpled to the cave floor again.

A voice rang out through the growing dimness. "Young lord! Do not harm yourself further!"

The creatures... one of them spoke! "What... what... Who are you?" William asked of the darkness. No more than a tiny spark now remained of the flashlight's former radiance. One of the creatures stood just slightly closer to William than the rest of the assemblage. As it raised a hand into the air, a soft, pure white glow illuminated the cave; like a slow lightning. The light was just as pure and just as white as the inferno that had struck him blind. Yet, the glowing brilliance seemed now to carry less force. Instead of a blinding beam, it flowed gently; bathing every inch of the cave in a brilliant yet gentle glow.

The creature again spoke; its voice much louder than its stature would suggest. "We are... friends, young lord. Please allow us to care for your injuries."

Two hundred eyes probed William's features as he asked, "What... what do you want?"

The creature replied, "As I have already stated, young lord, we wish to care for your injuries." The creature speaking wore a robe of sorts, and appeared to have a long white beard in addition to the tuft of hair on top of his head. William correctly judged him to be male. A small necklace of some sort hung around his neck and what appeared to be a drawstring pouch hung from his hip.

"Young lord," the creature continued, "we wish to help. Will you allow this?" Stepping to one side, he gestured to another creature to come forward. From some distance back into the crowd, there came a feminine looking creature carrying a small bowl. She slowly paced up beside the first creature and stopped, staring up at William.

I guess if they wanted to hurt me, William thought, *they'd have done it by now.* "Um, yeah... I guess," he said.

The female creature approached William, setting the bowl next to his feet. Studying her features, William noted that she had a kind face. "My name is Lucinda. I am the care giver," she said. "Please allow me to apply this medicine to your injuries." She wore a ghostly white robe without ornamentation, save a necklace displaying a rather dull looking pebble, similar to the one worn by the bearded creature. The velvety tuft of hair on her head was a deep chestnut brown. Glancing around at the assembled throng, William noted that their hair seemed to come in numerous shades of brown, black, and silvery-gray, in addition to white. Lucinda, aware that William's mind was wandering, spoke again. "I would like to be of assistance... may I please treat your injuries?"

William's gaze fell once again upon Lucinda. "What is it?" he asked. "It's not like... bat poop or anything like that, is it?"

"It contains a variety of herbs, young lord," she replied. "It will soothe the pain and speed your healing. Please show me your injuries." She picked her bowl up again and stood by while William used his one good arm to remove the boot and sock from his foot with the sprained ankle. Gingerly, Lucinda applied a small amount of the poultice and the pain faded. Within a few moments' time, the swelling had completely disappeared and it was as if he'd never sprained it.

"Wow!" William said, "Whatever that stuff is, it works great." He then offered his broken arm to Lucinda. She examined it briefly; a look of disappointment and deep concern spreading across her face. "Allow me first to treat your other injuries," she said, "This may require... other measures."

William agreed, and proceeded to awkwardly pull his pant legs up, exposing his kneecaps. For the first time, he was grateful that this particular pair of pants fit him so loosely. Lucinda applied the poultice to each in turn and the pain evaporated, just as it had with his ankle. She treated his other injuries, having the same effect, until she came again to his broken arm. "I am afraid, young lord, that this is beyond my medicine," she said. After a brief pause, she continued, "Please wait here a moment. I have to speak with Sador."

"Sador, who's that?" William asked.

"Sador, " Lucinda motioned to the bearded creature who held the glowing stone, "...is the elder. I must confer with him."

"Who... which one of you was I chasing when I fell?" William asked.

Lucinda replied, "That was Enid, my husband. He was too disturbed by the experience to be here. I must apologize on his behalf. He did not mean to cause you harm. Now, please remain here. I must confer with Sador."

As William did his best to get his sock and boot back on his foot, Lucinda paced over to Sador. As they met, both glanced briefly back at William and removed the tiny stones which hung around their necks. As they began to speak, William noticed that their voices had diminished to a point where they were now barely discernible. *Those necklaces,* William thought, *the pebbles must somehow amplify their voices.* After a moment, Sador handed off the glowing stone which he held to another creature who stood close by. As he did, the stone dimmed dramatically before flaring to life again. This captured William's curiosity. *I guess... maybe you've got to squeeze that one to make it glow. And the harder you squeeze, the brighter it glows.*

William could not make out any of what Lucinda and Sador were discussing. However, it was clear that it was an intense discussion. The flow of emotion was quite evident. Sador's head finally bowed and there was a long silence before he turned to face William again. He hung the pebble necklace around his neck once more and spoke. "Are you well enough to travel, young lord?"

"Why do you keep calling me that?" asked William. "My name is William... William Thornton."

Sador sighed, "We shall discuss that soon. Right now, I need to know if you can travel."

William carefully stood, cradling his right arm. "Well, I'm sure I can walk fine now, but I'll never get up that rope with this busted arm! And that crack in the wall over there is way too narrow for me to fit through."

"We will travel to our village," Sador began. "It is not far." As he said this, the hundred or so other creatures began filtering off, heading towards the passageway in the far corner. The cave began to grow dim as the creature holding the light emitting stone retreated down the passageway.

Sador removed a tiny stone from the pouch that hung from his hip. To William, it looked like a tiny bead of glass. As Sador squeezed the stone between his fingers, it flared to life, flooding the cave with radiance once again. "In our village," Sador concluded, "there is something that will bring you full healing... if you have the courage to do what is necessary." He said nothing more, but followed the throng of other creatures retreating into the depths. Somewhat hesitantly, William followed.

Blind My Eyes

Blind my eyes
that I may see
what truly is true.
Freedom flowers in bondage
and death of self
births life anew.

The bleakest night
gives way to light
when death's work is done.

The soul surrendered
the Savior remembers...
in loss, the prize is won.

Michael M. Middleton

from Modern Musings
copyright 2003

Chapter
Thirteen

William had to walk carefully in order to avoid
tripping over his untied boot laces, but as he followed Sador
down the widening passageway, he began to feel a little more
at ease. He could not imagine, however, what could be done
for his broken arm. Still, he was convinced by then that these
gray creatures, whatever they were, meant him no harm. He
decided to try to find out more about his tiny benefactors.
Trying his best to sound casual, he asked, "So, why do you
guys live down here... underground? Are you like... trolls, or
something?"

Confused by this mythological reference, Sador paused
before answering. "We are the *Ankara*, young lord. We live
here because we must... for now." There was a strange,
distant tone in Sador's words.

"Well, like... who... *what* are you?" William asked.
"Are you aliens, or leprechauns, or what?" he pressed.

It was obvious that these words meant nothing to
Sador. "Young lord, all of your questions will be answered, in
time. For now, let us care for your injury."

As Sador spoke, they emerged from the passageway into
a great room many times larger than the one where William
had fallen. Around the perimeter were dozens of little houses,
fashioned from wood and dry grass, woven together. As
William looked closer, he noticed that several homes
incorporated other materials, as well. Most of the dwellings

that were elevated on rock shelves had staircases made from Popsicle sticks or building blocks. Others utilized cotton swabs for a portion of their framework. And a few made use of such other small elements as pencils, paper clips, bottle tops, and wooden matchsticks.

Most of the houses had a small fire pit in front, with miniature cooking implements laid out neatly nearby. Two or three had what looked like seesaws fashioned out of old spoons alongside of them. None of the houses William could see appeared to have a door, only a drawn curtain covering the single entrance, which faced well-worn paths.

As they entered the village, Sador returned his light emitting stone to the pouch that hung from his side. It was no longer needed. In the middle of the great room was a pool of water some six feet across. A gentle glow rose from its depths like a gleaming pillar. It then spilled out in all directions, flooding the great chasm with soft light. Sador motioned to the luminous waters. "There you will find healing, " he said. "Drink from the *Pool of Truth,* and you shall be fully restored."

Watched by hundreds of eyes, William approached the gleaming pool. The water was perfectly clear, like the finest crystal. It was so clear that its depth was difficult to judge, but he guessed that it was twelve feet deep or more. Near the bottom, William could see openings in the wall several inches across, where he assumed that springs deeper in the earth fed the pool. He knew that water was feeding into the pool somehow, as the overflow spilled out of a side channel, forming a small stream that meandered across the floor of the cave and disappeared into the distance.

Wedged within the walls of the pool were seven gleaming stones. William did not know if they were there naturally or had been placed there, but he knew that they were being compressed somehow, as they emitted the steady, brilliant glow that filled the great cavern. He was so captivated by this sight that he nearly forgot about his broken arm. The pure radiance of the stones seemed to have somehow become one with the crystal waters; as if the two elements had become intermingled in some inseparable fashion.

Sador now stood beside William, and seemed to be reading his thoughts. "The two are one, young lord. As a husband and wife become one in marriage... and as the realm of flesh and that of spirit shall one day wed; so here in this place, the water of life... and the light of truth... are one."

"I don't understand," said William. "What *are* those glowing rocks? And that light... I've seen it before, in my dreams. What is this place?" Like a weakened dam finally breached, he now fairly burst with a torrent of inquisitions. "Who or *what* are you? And what are you doing here... underground... on my grandma's ranch?" William continued, "Are you guys responsible for all the weird stuff that's been happening since we moved here? And why do you keep calling me *young lord?*"

William suddenly felt a sharp pain in his shoulder, as if he'd been stung by a hornet. Before he had time to react, this was followed by two more piercings. Crying out in pain and fear, he spun around just in time to see a blur flying towards him. Instinctively, he threw his left hand up to shield his face. A spear about as long as a pencil buried itself deeply in the fleshy part of his hand. He shrieked in pain!

"Marshok!" Sador cried out in a thunderous voice. "Cease, this instant!" As Sador spoke, William's gaze fell upon his attackers. Perched on a wide ledge some thirty feet away were four of the gray creatures. Two were armed with bows and a prolific supply of arrows; while two others seemed to be operating some kind of a medieval instrument of war. They were just beginning to load another spear into this machine as Sador withdrew a light emitting stone from his pouch. He raised it high into the air, loosing an inferno of light. Shrieks of pain mingled with rage rang out from the tiny assailants as they fled.

Before William could fill the air with the fear and rage which now burned within him, Sador shouted to him in earnest. "Young lord, delay no longer! If you wish to leave this place alive, kneel down and drink, now!" William could not grasp why, but he knew that he must do as Sador commanded. He yanked the spear from his hand with his teeth and knelt down beside the gleaming pool.

As his lips reached for the healing waters, he saw something which nearly paralyzed him. There, reflected in the shining pool, he saw a dark and sinister being... himself. He was now quite literally face to face with the ugly, dark other-self he'd seen in the vision of the altar. Depraved declarations of vengeance and bitterness and self-serving manipulation radiated from his face like a black aura. Sador cried out from behind him, "Healing necessitates the acknowledgement of our need! Drink, young lord!" William had no idea what this statement had to do with him at that particular moment, but the urgency of the exhortation shook him enough to enflame his courage. His lips met the crystal water and he drank deeply.

It was as if life had become a tangible thing... a substance that could be ingested. Every fiber of William's being pulsated with energy and revelation. A deluge of conflicting emotions overcame him as he drank... despair and joy, fear and hope.

He had become suddenly aware of the dark thoughts and self-serving motivations that he had harbored within himself. He saw his bitterness and resentment for what it was; a sickness that he had carefully fostered over the years. This sickness served the diabolical and destructive cause of *self-justification*. His lower nature had treasured every injustice and every wounding inflicted upon it, for these served as excuses for every hurtful word, unkind deed, and hateful attitude he had leveled at others. It was like a self-loathing cancer that fed on pain.

Sincere grief over his own selfishness neared the point at which William felt that it would crush him. Just at the very brink of that point, however, there was a sudden release. The light of life that is found in the simple acknowledgement of what is true seeped into every pore of William's mind and spirit... and darkness simply dissolved.

William was now awash in an ecstasy that could not be described... only known. It was as if he had stumbled upon the very mystery of existence; as if he had discovered, in some tiny measure, the truth of what was always meant to be. For the first time, he felt truly whole and truly free. By acknowledging the reality of his own guilt, he had become innocent.

With an understanding that cannot be explained, William knew that he had just begun a journey. This journey would lead over glorious mountain peaks and through barren deserts. Many miles would be traveled while carrying the burden of sorrow, and his lower nature would never relent in its efforts to entice him back into darkness. He had taken but the first step of a long and treacherous journey. Many trials and much hardship lay ahead.

And yet, this was a beginning.

Chapter
Fourteen

William hardly noticed it when two of the gray creatures climbed onto his back to remove the tiny arrows from his shoulder. The sudden jolt of pain from the arrow's barbed tips being torn from his flesh caught his attention, however. "Ow! Hey!" He reflexively sat up, swatting at the pain. The gray creatures deftly leapt from his back and fled across the floor of the cave.

"You are lucky to be alive, young lord," Sador addressed him warmly. The tone of his voice grew more somber as he continued, "The dark ones frequently lace their weapons with a fast acting poison." The word *poison* made William's heart skip a beat. "But you have drunk deeply of the healing waters. You shall not perish."

As William silently rose to his feet, he particularly noted that the pain in his right arm had vanished. He held his arm up to examine it. It appeared to be completely healed! His eyes grew wide and his mouth dropped open slightly as he repeatedly squeezed his hand into a fist, testing the arm's strength. "But, how?" he stammered.

Sador replied, "That is but one of a thousand questions, I presume." He bowed his head for a moment as he continued, "Perhaps it is best if we start at the beginning." His head still bowed, Sador raised only his eyes to meet William's gaze. "You are about to know, " he paused, "something that no one of your kind has known... for more than a thousand years."

William was close to rupturing with anticipation as Sador continued, "Are you sure that you desire the responsibility of this knowledge?"

The words leapt uncontrollably from William's lips, "Heck, yeah!" He then felt suddenly embarrassed at having blurted out in such a manner. He quickly grasped for the noble, wisdom-seeking tone of voice that was used on all of the Kung-Fu movies he watched on Saturday mornings. "I mean... *'Yes, great teacher, I would like to understand...'*" That still didn't feel quite right, but William figured that he would let it go, rather than risk embarrassing himself further.

Sador now simply stared at him with a confused look on his face. It seemed as though anything outside of simple, direct sincerity perplexed him. "Um, please..." William said, meekly.

"In the beginning," Sador began. "Yes, let us begin in the beginning." He then drew in a slow, deep breath; like someone about to begin the telling of a very long story. As he began to speak, Sador's eyes gazed right through William, focusing on the memories of eons past. Scores of tiny villagers filtered out of their homes and away from their other occupations, slowly gathering around in silent homage to the recounting of this tale.

"In the beginning... the Great One created all things," he spoke quite slowly. "He first created the spirit realm; a place of glory and majesty... and inapproachable light. He then fashioned the material world as its reflection. Remember this, young lord," he addressed William directly, "That which eyes of flesh may perceive is but a reflection; an echo... no more than a foretaste of that which is truly real." Sador paused, and then continued, "The Great One has purposed from the beginning that these two realms would one day wed and become one... together to become a more glorious creation than either could be on its own." William listened intently, trying to understand the meaning of this imagery.

"You see, William," Sador called him by name now, "The ultimate purpose of the Great One, the Lord of lords, has always been to attain a counterpart... a reflection of Himself... a bride. You, young lord, are a tiny portion of that bride." This was beginning to sound strangely familiar to William.

"It is for this purpose, and this purpose alone," Sador continued, "that untold billions of stars now burn in the deep heavens.." William slowly nodded, indicating that he understood, at least in a limited way. "When this world was framed," Sador's eyes grew wide with memories of wonder, "such glory as you have never imagined filled the air, the land, the sea. The very atmosphere was saturated with the music of the stars."

Aware that his thoughts and words were beginning to drift, Sador refocused himself. "All of these wonders were fashioned for the benefit of the creation that would grow into His bride. You, William, as I have already stated, are a tiny portion of that bride. We, the *Ankara*, were created along with man to serve as a dim reflection of your race. We were created for the purpose of helping you to understand yourselves and to help you understand the Great One's care for you, through the experience of caring for us. Mankind was given full dominion over the earth and *all* of its creatures, including the Ankara. We therefore refer to your race as the *lords of the earth*, as this is an accurate representation of the Great One's mandate. And," he smiled at William, "this is why we have referred to you as a *young lord*."

Sador paused to allow all of this to sink in before continuing. "All was beauty and joy in the beginning. The Lord of lords fashioned seven great fountains that rose from the depths, forming streams of living water, which ran throughout the earth. Instantaneous healing of any infirmity was readily available to all. But after darkness entered the human race with Adam's fall, each generation became more deeply stained with sin. As you have seen for yourself, there

133

is a price attached to the healing which the water brings; the acknowledgement of one's need. It was the Great One's desire that the water of life should provide healing for both body *and* *spirit*. In order for this healing to occur, one must be willing to see and acknowledge their need.

As each generation of mankind grew darker and more depraved, they became unwilling to admit this need, and thus unable to be healed. As mankind's self-loathing sickness spread, your kind persecuted the Ankara mercilessly!" Sador's words, though passionate, directed no malice at William.

"You see," he began again, "sin produces self-hatred. Being your reflection, it was inevitable that this hatred would overflow onto us... a most convenient target. Untold millions of our kind were held captive and slowly tormented to death for the amusement of those infected by the insanity that darkness breeds." William now felt a deep sense of regret and shame. Could these things really be true? As a child of Adam, could such a vile potential reside within him?

Sador's voice rose slightly, as his tale reached its first climax. "When this cancer of hatred had spread throughout the human race, the Great One declared an end. Driven half mad with grief, He decided to purge creation of this infection." Sador motioned to an attendant who held several scrolls. The attendant paced over to Sador, who selected one of them and unrolled it. Holding the scroll in front of him, he began, "As the Great Book declares:

1 Then the Lord saw that the wickedness of man was great in the earth, and that every intent of the thoughts of his heart was only evil continually. And the Lord was sorry that he had made man on the earth, and He was grieved in His heart. So the Lord said, "I will destroy man whom I have created from the face of the earth, both man and beast, creeping thing and birds of the air, for I am sorry that I have made them."

As Sador paused, a swarm of revelation overtook William. "You're... you're talking about the flood, aren't you? You know, Noah... big boat... lots of animals?"

Sador nodded in agreement. "Yes, young lord. I see that you are somewhat familiar with the Great Book. The Lord of lords did manage to find one among your race that had not been fully consumed by the darkness. You have named him. Through this one man, He would preserve a remnant of His creation." Sador unrolled the scroll a bit more and continued.

*2 *Noah was six hundred years old when the flood of waters was on the earth. So Noah, his wife, and his son's wives went into the ark because of the waters of the flood. Of clean beasts, of beasts that are unclean, of birds, and of everything that creeps on the earth, two by two they went into the ark to Noah, male and female, as God had commanded Noah. And it came to pass after seven days that the waters of the flood were on the earth. In the six-hundredth year of Noah's life, in the second month, the seventeenth day of the month, on that day all the fountains of the great deep were broken up, and the windows of heaven were opened. And the rain was on the earth forty days and forty nights.*

*1 Genesis 6:5-7 NKJV
*2 Genesis 7: 6-12 NKJV

Sador rolled the scroll back up and handed it to the attendant. He then turned to William once again. "And so, the earth was purged from the wickedness of man... for a time," he said. "Along with the torrential rain, the Great One broke up the fountains of the great deep, flooding the Earth. The pool that you stand before is a remnant of one of those fountains."

"You mean...wow!" William said. "Is that how all of those guys in the Bible used to live so long? I always thought those numbers were typos or something. I wondered if Noah was really six hundred years old when the flood came."

"Yes, William, this water has the capacity to vastly extend one's life," Sador replied. "But even it, glorious as it is, is but a reflection. The true *water of life* is a seed... a seed which is planted in one's spirit when they confess their need and are restored to fellowship with the Great One; the Lord of lords."

"I think I understand," William said.

Sador continued, "This seed lies buried deeply within each who has become a recipient of grace. It will remain hidden there, slowly transforming the mind and spirit, until the Great Day."

"*The Great Day?*" asked William.

"When the Lord of lords returns to establish the Eternal Kingdom," Sador explained. "On that day, that truly glorious day," he continued, "Heaven and Earth shall wed... and become one. God's very presence will saturate everything, and darkness will be put away forever! The creation of God will be eternally restored to that which it was always intended to be."

There was a long silence as the magnificence of this statement reverberated through every heart and mind. Then, Sador continued. "After the great flood, mankind once again multiplied and spread across the face of the Earth. Soon, darkness had once again enticed your race and we once again found ourselves the targets of hideous persecution. As hatred and violence grew once more, the Lord of lords divided the earth into seven great land masses*1 in order to slow its progress; each continent sheltering the remnant of one of the fountains of the great deep. We, the Ankara, took refuge from man's persecution in the deep places of the Earth and the Great One gave us the task of protecting and caring for what remains of the fountains of living water. When the Great Day arrives, they shall be restored to their former glory and purpose." From memory, Sador once again quoted from the Great Book, "*for the Lamb who is in the midst of the throne will shepherd them and lead them to living fountains of waters. And God will wipe away every tear from their eyes.*" *2

Sensing that he had finished speaking, William asked, "Sador, may I ask a few questions?"

"Certainly, young lord," he warmly replied.

"Those glowing rocks... what do you call them?" William inquired. "I've never seen anything like them before."

"They are *Shekinah stones,*" Sador replied. "The light which they emit is a dim reflection of the Shekinah of God; the all consuming glory which emanates from His very presence."

"A *dim* reflection?" William quipped. "You've gotta' be kidding!"

"No flesh could survive the absolute purity of the true Shekinah," Sador replied. "Even the great prophet Moses, for his own safety, was only allowed to see a glimpse of the Great One's back as he passed by on the mountain. And the apostle Paul was struck blind and nearly incinerated by the briefest glimpse of the risen Lord's glory. Not until the Great Day, when darkness has been fully purged, will any survive such an encounter."

William could form no concept of such a thing, but simply accepted it for the time being. "Well, those necklaces..." he began.

"As you have probably already guessed," Sador interrupted, "the *sound stones* they contain greatly amplify sound. They enable us to communicate over much greater distances than we otherwise could."

"Cool!" William replied.

Sador spoke again, "The Great One has also provided us with many other special gifts, such as *fire stones*." He withdrew two small stones from the pouch that hung from his side and held them up for William to see. "When two are struck together, the surfaces which make contact generate a tremendous heat for a moment or two."

"So! That must be what happened to that mouse trap!" William concluded. "I thought that spring looked like it had been melted..." He paused, then shyly said, "Um, sorry about that, by the way. I'll never set another mouse trap again, I promise!"

"Yes, we do not spend all of our time underground," another of the Ankara interjected. "We do venture out at night to forage for food and building materials, and such useful discarded items as we may find." William stared at this stranger, thinking that he somehow looked familiar. "I am Enid," he said. "I am grateful that you have fully recovered from your injuries." He then bowed his head slightly and sheepishly concluded, "I did not mean to cause you harm."

*1 see Genesis 10:25, I Chronicles 1:19 *2 Revelations 7:17 NKJV

"Um, no problem," William replied. "It was really kinda' my fault." A new thought entered William's mind and his voice now took on a darker tone. "But who was that who shot me with the arrows?" He asked, pointedly. "Who is Marshok?"

"Marshok," Enid's voice quivered with a peculiar mixture of both anger and grief, "was once my brother."

"*Was* your brother?" William asked. "What do you mean *was*?"

"He has become one of the dark ones," Enid replied coldly.

Sador noted the question in William's eye as Enid paced sadly away. "You see, young lord," he began, "as the end of the age of darkness approaches, the sickness of sin has begun to infect even a few among the Ankara. Marshok has become one of the dark ones. Consumed by hatred, anger, and resentment, they refuse to embrace the healing that comes from the pool of truth. Instead, they embrace the darkness and seek to spread pain and destruction wherever they can. They bear a particularly strong resentment towards your race, young lord, and constantly plot new ways of doing harm to mankind."

"You mean, like gremlins?" William inquired.

Again, this reference meant nothing to Sador. "We know that they have been responsible for certain outbreaks of disease," he began. "And they occasionally cause destructive fires and the like. In recent days, Marshok and those he leads have been staging a series of raids on this village; stealing a great number of sound stones and fire stones. They have been very methodical... and we are convinced that they are planning something diabolical. We do not yet know what this is, however."

"What's he so angry about?" William asked. "Everyone here seems so nice..."

"When Marshok was young, he made a habit of holding on to small hurts," Sador replied. "Over time, his heart grew heavy and dark with this burden." He sighed deeply, and then continued, "When the time came for him to wed, he asked Lucinda to join with him. But she loved Marshok's brother, Enid, and chose him instead. Marshok gave in to the anguish and rage that he had fostered within himself over the years and became fully consumed by the darkness. The night before Enid and Lucinda were to be wed, he set fire to Lucinda's dwelling and stole away to join a band of the dark ones. Since that night, the darkness within him has grown to such a point that he has now become their leader."

William did not know what to say in response to such a sad tale. He just stood there, silently. Suddenly, a tiny trumpet rang out across the great cavern. "It is near sunset," Sador announced. "You should be getting home now."

"Oh, right..." William said, suddenly realizing that he hadn't had any idea what time of day it was.

As William bent down to tie his boot laces, Sador calmly said, "You are welcome to visit this place again, if you would like. However, I must insist that you do not share with anyone the fact of our existence."

"Yeah, I understand," William replied. "Besides, if I said anything, they'd probably just lock me away..." He finished tying his boot and returned hurriedly through the long passageway to where his rope dangled from the room above, Enid lighting his way with a Shekinah stone.

Retrieving his gear, he ascended the rope to the fort. He then quickly untied the rope from the leg of the couch and tossed it aside. Finally, he dragged the couch back across the floor so that its proximity to the opening would not betray its existence to Sharon or anyone else who might stumble upon the cave. "I'll find some kind of a way to hide this hole," he assured Enid, "so that no one else discovers it."

Exiting the cave just after sunset, William quickly made his way over to where Chester was still tied. "Sorry I was gone so long," he said. "I'll bet you're thirsty..." William removed the lid from his canteen and held it up to the horse's mouth. Dusty nostrils flared wide as the horse caught the scent of the cool water. William coaxed the horse's chin high into the air so that its head tilted back slightly and then slowly emptied the canteen. Chester did his best to lap up what he could of it.

When the canteen was empty, William untied Chester from the great oak tree and swung up into the saddle. "Home, boy!" he said, prodding the horse into a pace just slightly faster than he was comfortable with. Together they crested the dusty knoll and raced the darkness home.

Chapter Fifteen

William was so overwhelmed by his experience that day that it was some time before he accepted Sador's invitation to visit the Ankara village again. However, he did keep the promise he'd made to Enid about concealing the passageway he'd created in the back wall of the fort. The morning following his first visit to the Ankara, he devised a plan and returned to the fort.

He first asked to borrow some tools from the tractor barn. "Sure boy, use whatever you'd like," Mary said. "Just be sure to put things back where you found them when you're done."

Emptying the prior contents of his backpack, he slipped in a claw hammer and a rusty old saw which hung on the back wall of the barn. Searching a number of dusty shelves, he located an old mayonnaise jar filled with a variety of nails. He placed this in his backpack as well.

The realization then hit him that the glass jar would probably shatter as it rattled against the hammer inside the backpack. He removed the jar from the backpack, set it aside, and thought for as moment. *Well, I'm going to need a blanket, or a sheet, or something anyway...*

Leaving his backpack where it lay, William began to take a survey of the barn's contents. He searched through a number of cabinets and storage bins, but this effort proved fruitless. He did find quite a few cleaning rags and old towels, but nothing came even close to the size that he needed.

Then, he remembered all of his family's stuff that was in storage up in the loft. *I'll bet I can find something that'll work up there,* he thought.

He climbed the steep staircase leading up to the loft. About half of the elevated platform was occupied by various boxes, crates, and a few miscellaneous pieces of furniture which they had no use for at that point. Draping over his dad's old recliner was a large quilt that had been used to protect his mom's full-length mirror during the move from Reno. *That's perfect!* he thought. Pulling the quilt from the recliner, he tossed it over the side of the loft and paced back down the staircase to the ground level.

He then dragged the quilt over to his backpack. He wrapped the jar of nails up in the quilt and began stuffing it into the backpack. However, it soon became evident that it was far too big to fit. *I guess I'll just have to carry the quilt by itself,* he concluded.

Removing the jar from the quilt, he wrapped it in a couple of old towels he'd found, instead. He then stuffed the padded jar into the backpack. Folding the quilt, he looked around the barn again and gathered a half a dozen or so discarded two-by-fours and a few other scrap pieces of lumber. These, he tightly bundled together with bailing wire.

William now took stock of his growing pile of supplies, running through a mental checklist. *Hmmm, needs something else...* he thought. Surveying the shelves again, he spotted a stack of a dozen old license plates and a shiny chrome hubcap. He retrieved these and barely managed to stuff them into his backpack. Zipping the backpack closed again proved to be quite a task, but he managed it after several minutes of trying. Realizing that he hadn't yet asked permission to ride Chester again, William returned to the house in order to do so. It was almost lunchtime, so after getting permission to ride Chester, he stayed to eat before returning to the tractor barn.

He moved the backpack, quilt, and scrap lumber next door to the horse barn, and then called Chester in from the pasture, leading him to where the saddle and other supplies were kept. After saddling Chester, he draped the quilt over the horse's hindquarters, strapping it in place with a pair of rawhide ties that hung from the back of the saddle.

After several minutes of deliberation over how to transport the lumber, he came up with a workable plan. He tied one end of a long rope to the saddle horn. He then tied the other end around the bundled lumber, cinching it tightly. After swinging up into the saddle, he braced the rope over his shoulder and across the top of his backpack. He'd decided that he would drag the lumber along the path out to the fort. It wasn't exactly comfortable for William or the horse, but he figured that it would get the job done.

Enduring several choruses of "What in the world is that boy up to now?" he began his trek out to the fort. Mary met him at the pasture gate, opening it to let him through. He responded to her inquisitions with, "I just wanted to spruce up the fort a bit, Grandma."

After a somewhat difficult ride, William dismounted near the mouth of the cave. He untied the rope from the saddle horn and removed the quilt from Chester's back before leading the horse over to the now familiar oak tree. He tied Chester to a low hanging branch and returned to the cave. Picking up the bundle of lumber, he tossed it through the opening. It tumbled nearly all the way to the bottom.

He then draped the quilt across his shoulder and followed the lumber down into the fort. When he reached the floor of the cave, he took hold of the rope that was attached to the lumber. He dragged the bundle across the floor to the back wall.

He next removed the quilt and backpack from his shoulders, setting them aside. Untying the bundle of lumber, he laid the boards out on the floor of the cave. When his eyes had sufficiently adjusted to the dimness, he laid the lumber out in a crisscrossing pattern. Removing the other supplies from his backpack, he nailed the boards together; forming a crude frame somewhat taller and wider than the hole he'd chiseled in the back wall of the fort.

He used the saw he'd brought along to trim off the few overhanging ends of lumber before laying the quilt out on top of the frame. He then nailed the quilt in place, forming a wall of sorts. Next, he flipped the frame over and nailed the leftover quilt material to the back side. Finally, he stood this new creation up and placed it in front of the hole in the back wall of the cave. The fit was perfect; it covered the hole completely.

Now, William dragged the couch over, placing it against the makeshift wall. After using the chrome hubcap and old license plates to decorate the new backdrop, he returned the tools and jar of nails to his backpack. Pacing across the floor of the cave, he admired his work from a distance. *Not bad,* he thought. *It does kinda' brighten the place up a bit. And no one would think to look behind it.*

Satisfied that he had completed his task, William collected his backpack and climbed back out of the cave. He crossed the dusty field, untied Chester from the oak tree, and swung up into the saddle. He knew that he would want to visit the Ankara village again, but not right away. He was simply too overloaded with revelation for the time being. He'd been profoundly disturbed by the vision of his lower nature that he had seen at the *Pool of Truth.* His heart and mind simply needed time to process things.

After arriving at home, William unsaddled Chester and returned him to the pasture. William himself then returned to the house and indulged in an afternoon shower before playing a few games of pool. After dinner, he read a couple of chapters from *The Beast Within* before going to bed a bit earlier than usual.

Chapter Sixteen

For the next couple of weeks, William spent most of his time hanging around the house. He played a lot of pool and finished reading *The Beast Within*. Wanting something more to read, he searched the bookshelves in the game room, but didn't find much else to his liking. He found himself paging through his grandma's old magazines and watching a lot of television.

William's level of boredom grew with the passing days. Other than his egg duties, there just didn't seem to be much to do. He'd tried to fish the pond again a couple of times, but as the summer days grew hotter, the fishing grew poor. He thought of visiting the Ankara again, but just wasn't ready.

Although he enjoyed the quiet, open spaces, William had not yet fully acclimated to living in the country. He found himself missing his old friends terribly. Back in Reno, many of his best friends lived within just a few blocks of him. There was a terrific park just down the street where they would all meet after school to hang out. And on Saturdays, they would organize neighborhood-wide games of kickball. If all else failed, there was an ice cream shop about a ten minute bike ride away that had a couple of pinball games in the back corner. He could always count on running into one or two of his friends there.

Now however, the only other kid his age close enough to visit was Sharon Stewart. And this was simply out of the question. He'd begun to really look forward to Sundays. It was the one day of the week that he got to see other kids. Also, he could usually talk his dad into buying lunch at the Big Boy drive-in just down the street from the church.

Late one evening, just as he was about to drift off to sleep, William heard a strangely familiar scratching sound. He cracked his eyelids and twitched his head to one side, listening to the darkness. For a moment or two, he heard nothing but crickets and coyotes. Just as his eyelids were about to close again, a familiar voice called out from his windowsill. "William," Enid began. "Are you awake?"

William quickly rolled over and sat up, facing the open window. In the far corner, silhouetted by a nearly full moon, stood Enid. Next to him was a saddled kangaroo rat. For some strange reason, this sight no longer seemed so odd. "Enid!" William greeted him, "It's good to see you. What are you up to?"

"Good evening, William," Enid replied. "A few of us were out collecting food and I thought that I would pay you a visit. I didn't wake you, did I?"

"No," William said. "Well, almost… but it's ok. I've been kinda' bored lately. How have you been?"

Enid tied the kangaroo rat's reigns to the shaft of a nail that protruded from the windowsill and jumped down, taking a seat near the foot of the bed. The two of them became fast friends, as they talked long into the night.

William learned much about the Ankara that night. As he had suspected, Enid shared the fact that English was not their primary language. When William asked how they had learned to speak English, Enid simply replied, "We are a very observant race, young lord. We watch. We listen." He recited a few passages from the Great Book in his native tongue, as

William listened in fascination. To William, the Ankara language sounded something like a cross between Greek and Gaelic. It had a very musical quality to it.

Enid also shared much about the Ankara history and culture. He told William of the musical instruments they constructed from natural materials and of the games their children played... and of many wondrous treasures they had discovered in the deep places of the Earth that were still unknown to man. He also told William many of the details of their daily lives, such as the food they ate. This consisted mostly of wild grains, fruit, and a few varieties of edible greens such as dandelion, lamb's quarters, and shepherd's purse. Occasionally, they also constructed traps to catch small fish.

"And..." William prodded, glancing towards the open door of his room, "The night you were in the kitchen?

Enid seemed to read his thoughts. "Yes, William, we do occasionally scavenge through human dwellings for small amounts of supplemental food stuffs, such as dried beans or rice... or other such useful things as we may find discarded by your kind."

"Well, Grandma still sets the mouse traps," William warned. "How 'bout I just leave some stuff out for you on my windowsill here from time to time?" Enid smiled, thanking William for his kindness.

The moon rose high as the hours passed. Finally, William grew too tired to stay awake any longer. As his eyes grew heavy, Enid rose to leave. "I should be getting home now, " he said, "or Lucinda may be disturbed." He climbed up onto the windowsill, untying the kangaroo rat. As he mounted its back, he asked, "It is your birthday tomorrow, is it not?"

Surprised, William asked, "How did you know that?"

"We are an observant race!" Enid chuckled. "We watch, we listen..."

"Well, yes," William replied. "I turn twelve tomorrow."

"Such an occasion is worthy of a gift," Enid declared. He removed the small drawstring pouch that hung from his side and tossed it to William.

William thanked Enid, setting the pouch on his nightstand. He then assured him that he would come to visit the village again soon. As Enid bounded from the windowsill and began the journey home, William's head reached hungrily for his pillow. He was soon fast asleep.

Chapter
Seventeen

William's twelfth birthday finally arrived. It was nearly nine-thirty when he awoke, his hair damp and beads of sweat glistening on his forehead. The Sun was already high in a cloudless sky and shone hot through his window.

It was a bead of sweat that woke him, as it streamed down the side of his face. As his eyes opened, William reflexively shielded his face from the light and sat up. After a quick stretch and a glance at his alarm clock, he sprung out of bed, surprised that he had slept so late.

A familiar scent lingered in the morning air. *All right!* he thought. *Strawberry muffins!* The enticement of his grandma's famous strawberry muffins hastened the completion of his morning routine. He quickly got dressed for the day, making only a haphazard attempt at brushing his teeth.

Conscious of it being his twelfth birthday, however, William did linger in front of the mirror for several moments, attempting to discern how long it might be before he could start shaving. A slender line of thin, dark hair across his upper lip convinced him that soon, he would be a man. *Maybe I'll grow sideburns,* he thought. *Yeah, that'd be cool!* He spent several more moments studying his now officially pre-teen visage.

Finally, the anxious, hollow feeling in William's stomach drew him away from the mirror. The scent of the freshly baked muffins had infested his nostrils again and he was drawn inexorably towards its source. Upon entering the dining room, he spied a large basket on the table containing the cherished muffins. Leaning against the basket, a note read, *Happy birthday, William. Your granny loves you!*

A stack of plates lay next to the basket. William placed four or five muffins on the top plate and carried it into the kitchen. *I'll need milk to go with these,* he thought.

Mary was seated at her regular spot by the window with the blue curtains. She was sipping a cup of coffee while paging through the latest issue of *Reader's Digest.* "Good morning, boy!" she greeted him as he entered the room. "Come here and let your grandma give you a birthday hug!"

William set the plate of muffins on the counter next to the refrigerator as he replied, "Good morning, Grandma. Thanks for the muffins!" He paced over and gave her a hug.

"Oh! Not so hard, boy!" she groaned. "You'll break my back!"

William released his grip and walked back over to the counter. He pulled a glass from the cupboard and filled it with milk from the refrigerator. Turning his back to the counter, he rested his weight against it and began consuming the still warm muffins. Following a rather long sip of chilled milk, he asked, "Where's Mom and Dad at?"

"Oh, they ran into town to pick up some ice," Mary answered. "They should be pulling in any time."

"Ice?" William inquired.

"Yep," Mary replied. "We're going on a picnic today. They ran into town to pick up a bag or two of ice for the cooler... probably grab some drinks and stuff, too."

"Where are we going?" William asked.

"We're heading up the road to Slide Rock," Mary replied.

William pressed, "*Slide Rock...* what's that?"

She answered, "It's a state park up north... near Flagstaff. There's a natural waterslide of sorts there... a spot in the streambed that's been worn into a smooth channel you can slide down. It's pretty fun for you young folks. Better dig out your swim trunks."

"Sounds cool, "William said, finishing his last bite of muffin. He gulped down the last of his milk and concluded, "I'll pull them out after I get the eggs."

"Don't bother, boy," Mary interrupted him in mid-stride, "I collected them for you already. A fella' shouldn't have to work on his birthday."

"Wow, thanks Grandma," William replied.

A voice called out from the doorway leading into the dining room. "Hey there, sleepy head! It's about time you crawled out of the tomb!"

Surprised and confused by the voice, William spun around. His older sister stood there in the doorway. "Leslie!" he erupted. "Where did you come from?"

"Hey, little worm," she quipped, "you didn't think I'd miss the big birthday, did you? I've got a few days off... I pulled in late last night."

"So..." William began slyly, "what did you bring me?"

"Yeah, I missed you too!" she chuckled.

Just about then, the front door opened. Jacob and Theresa walked in. Jacob carried two large bags of ice and a sack of groceries. As he and Theresa entered the dining room on their way to the kitchen, Leslie turned to greet them. "Hi, Mom! Hi Dad!"

"Good morning, sweetie," Theresa replied. " Is your brother up yet?"

Glancing back over her shoulder at William, she replied, "Yeah, he's in here. The little worm hit me up for presents already!"

"Well, it *is* my birthday," he muttered.

After setting the ice and groceries down, Jacob retrieved a large cooler from the utility room. Setting it on the kitchen counter, he emptied the two large bags of ice into the cooler and then placed the sodas they'd bought at the store in as well. He then placed the lid on top of the cooler and determined to stay out of the way until the ladies had prepared the rest of the food for the picnic. "Come on boy," he jested, "let's go shoot some pool while the women-folk do their thing."

While Jacob and William strode off towards the game room, Theresa, Leslie, and Mary prepared their lunches for the day. When everything was ready, Jacob was called back into the kitchen to carry the cooler out to the car. William carried a separate basket containing napkins, silverware, and the like. Fearing that a full size birthday cake might not survive the trip to the park, Mary had made cupcakes instead. She carried these with her as she followed everyone else outside.

"Mom and I can take all the food in my car," Leslie offered. "There's plenty of room in the back seat and we can catch up on things that way."

"Ok, honey," Jacob replied. "If you get there before we do, just hang out in the parking lot and we'll all pick out a good spot together." After loading the picnic supplies into the back seat of Leslie's car, Jacob, William, and Mary returned to the other car and took their seats. As Jacob slid in behind the steering wheel, he turned to William and said, "We'll be there in about an hour."

"Oh, nuts!" William exclaimed, "I forgot swim trunks!" He undid his seatbelt and had begun to open the car door when Jacob interrupted him.

"Woh there, boy! Your mom took care of that already. You've got swim trunks and a towel in the trunk." Wiping the sweat from his forehead, Jacob concluded, "Good thing, too. It's gonna' be a hot one. Should be a great day for swimming.

Roll that window down the rest of the way, why don't ya'?"
William closed the door, refastened his seatbelt, and rolled his
window down as far as it would go.

After about an hour's drive north, they came to Slide
Rock State Park. A pleasant lunch was followed by a couple
of hours of swimming in the chilly waters of Oak Creek. After
everyone had a chance to cool off and let lunch settle, they
returned to the picnic area for the cake-and-presents portion
of the birthday outing.

As William devoured the first of several cupcakes he
would eat that afternoon, Jacob retrieved the stash of presents
that had been hidden underneath a blanket in the trunk of the
car. William's eyes grew wide and inquisitive as the brightly
wrapped gifts were laid out across a neighboring picnic table.
That one must be the b.b. gun, he thought, eyeing a package
about three feet long and eight inches wide. It was wrapped
in paper displaying a variety of old-west scenery and seemed
to William to be pretty close to the dimensions of the
packaged b.b. guns he'd seen at the sporting goods store in the
mall.

Next to this package sat another about the size of a
large lunchbox. Several other gifts of various sizes soon
joined these two on the picnic table. As was his peculiar
tradition, Jacob arranged the gifts in order of size, small to
large. To William's chagrin, the one he assumed to be a b.b.
gun was the last in line; thus, the last he would get to open.

As Jacob finished arranging the gifts, he gave William
the nod to begin opening them as Theresa made sure her
camera was ready to start taking pictures. Vainly hoping that
he would get away with it, William walked directly to the
large box at the end of the line.

"No you don't, Mister!" Jacob cut him short. "You know
the routine."

Nuts! William thought, pacing back to the other end of the table. He picked up a small rectangular box, testing its weight in his hand. A note scribbled on the outside read, *From Dad.* Tearing it open, he discovered a neatly boxed three-blade pocketknife. Holding it up for the camera, he said, "Cool! Thanks, Dad!"

The next gift was a fancy leather wallet from his grandma with ten dollars inside. "All right! Thanks, Grandma!" he said, as he stuffed the wallet into his pocket and moved on. The next gift, a model car, was also from his grandma. As he worked his way farther down the line of gifts, William unwrapped a fancy pair of sunglasses, a stack of comic books, a selection of dress socks and ties, several new shirts and pairs of pants, and a new tackle box containing a few new lures and other fishing supplies.

Finally, he came to the last gift. Mary tellingly looked away as he glanced in her direction. However, confusion and disappointment quickly replaced glee as he tore the package open. Instead of the long-awaited b.b. gun, it was a new rod and reel set. "...top of the line," his dad assured him.

Jacob handed him a small, square piece of paper as he stared down at the gift. "Here boy, stick this in your new wallet," he said. "Now that you're twelve, you need a license to fish. Don't lose it."

"Um, thanks, Dad," William replied meekly. "It's really a neat pole."

"So, what do ya' say we get up real early tomorrow and pull some fish out of the river?" Jacob asked.

William brightened a little. "Sure Dad, that'd be great!"

After they returned home that evening and finished carrying everything inside, Jacob called his son out to the living room. "Yeah Dad," William replied as he entered the room. "What is it?"

"Well," Jacob began, "there's one present you didn't get to open yet."

"Huh?" asked William. "What's that?"

"Well, you see…" Jacob continued as he pulled a large wrapped package from behind the couch, "you can't have these in state parks, so we figured we'd wait until we got home to give it to you."

William lunged forward, snatching the package from his father's hands. It looked to be the right size. It felt like it was the right weight… Greedily, he shredded the gift-wrap, divorcing it from the package underneath in record time. Cradled there in his hands was the coolest looking b.b. gun he'd ever seen!

Fishing

A flick and a zip
drops the lad's lure
on water white as cream.

A streak of silver,
splashed with pine and peach,
slices through the frantic stream.

A lunge and a tug,
a stripping of line
fulfills the young boy's dream.

Michael M. Middleton

from Modern Musings
copyright 2003

Chapter
Eighteen

William's dad woke him a few minutes before 5 A.M. the next morning. "Come on, sleepy boy!" he crowed, shaking William's shoulder. "We're burning daylight."

William rolled over, cracking his eyelids. "What?" he huffed, sleepily. Then, rubbing his face and yawning deeply, he said, "Oh yeah, fishing... right."

"Leslie said that she would do your egg collection today," Jacob began. "I guess the big city girl wants to get in a little bit of *country* before she heads home."

William began to acknowledge his dad verbally, but was interrupted by another yawn. He nodded his acknowledgement instead.

"Okay, well... just put some clothes on and get your fishing stuff ready," Jacob cheerfully concluded. "I'll be in the kitchen throwing us together a quick breakfast. There's supposed to be cooler weather blowing in, so it ought to be really good fishing today."

As Jacob turned and headed for the kitchen, William sat up on his knees, bracing his elbows on the windowsill. Inhaling the crisp morning air, he took in the exotic pre-dawn colors. A very thin yellowish-orange line hugged the horizon. This melted into a light shade of aqua, unlike anything he'd seen before. Further up into the sky, the aqua took on a tinge of green, before deepening to an odd color somewhere between blue and black. *Sure do have some strange sunrises here,* he thought.

Turning from the window, William climbed down from his bed and shuffled off towards the bathroom. He clicked on the light, squinting while his eyes adjusted to the brightness. He then groggily brushed his teeth and splashed a little cold water on his face before returning to his bedroom.

There, he pulled clothes from the closet and got dressed for the day. It took him a moment to remember where he had left his wallet, which contained his first official fishing license… one of the many rites of passage leading towards manhood. Retrieving the wallet from the top of his dresser, he then collected the fishing pole and tackle box he'd received for his birthday from where they sat near the foot of his bed. On the way out to the kitchen, he recalled his new pocketknife. Spotting it on the nightstand, he paced back over and plopped it into his pants pocket. He stood there for a moment, until he was reasonably sure that he wasn't forgetting anything else. Satisfied, he sauntered off towards the kitchen.

On the way, he paused at the front door. Opening the door, he set his tackle box on the porch just outside. He then leaned his pole against the side of the house next to the tackle box. Closing the door again, he continued on to the kitchen.

As he entered the kitchen, Jacob was setting a used frying pan into the sink. He turned on the water, filling the pan, and added a little soap. "This'll have to, uh, soak for awhile," he began. "The first batch of bacon… got a little done."

A thick layer of gray, greasy smoke hugged the ceiling. William paced over to the window with the blue curtains, unlatching it and pushing it open. "You're dangerous, Dad!" he quipped. "Not as bad as Mom, but still pretty dangerous!"

"Unless you want to be getting your breakfast through an I.V.," Jacob jested, "you had better cut out the wise cracks!"

"Well, if you're gonna' have a grease fire," William retorted as he took his seat, "a house that's one big pile of logs isn't the smartest place to do it!"

Jacob dropped a plate of bacon and eggs in front of his son. "Scrambled okay?" he asked, ignoring William's last comment.

"Sure, fine..." William replied. "Can you grab the *Tabasco* when you go back for the toast?"

Jacob nodded and returned to the counter by the sink. He collected two sets of silverware, the toast he'd prepared, and a large bottle of *Tabasco* brand pepper sauce. After placing these on the small table by the window where William sat in eager anticipation, he finally returned for his own plate of food. After wolfing down their breakfast, father and son placed their dishes in the sink and headed for the car. "Just toss your stuff in the back seat with mine," Jacob instructed as he opened the driver's side door. "Did you remember your fishing license?"

"Sure did," William chirped. "What kind of fish are we going after, anyway?"

Jacob latched his seatbelt and turned the key. A few pumps on the gas pedal, and the car roared to life. "Oh, a few different kinds," he answered. "There's trout, of course. And small-mouth bass, sunfish, and some pretty decent crappie. Sometimes you'll pull a catfish out of one of the deeper holes."

William latched his seatbelt and pulled the car door shut. From a small cooler in the back seat came a sound akin to popcorn popping. William curiously glanced over his shoulder as Jacob shifted the car into gear and asked, "Um, Dad... what's that?"

"What's *what*?" Jacob pressed.

"I think there's something alive in the lunch box!" William declared.

"Oh! That's not lunch, silly boy!" Jacob chuckled. "Well, not *our* lunch, anyway. I caught a few crickets last night to use for bait. I dug a few worms out of the garden, too."

"Crickets?" William asked. "Live crickets?"

"Nothin' better for trout!" Jacob assured him. "They work pretty good for bass, too. And if you want to try for a catfish, you've gotta' have a worm on your line. Little cubes of hot dog on a small hook work really well for crappie, so I threw in a couple of them, as well."

"Well, I might try the hot dog thing," William said, "but as for the bugs and worms… I think I'll just stick to spinners and spoons."

A few minutes of travel down the bumpy country lane brought them to a wide turnout a short walk from the banks of the Agua Fria River. Jacob pulled the car over under a cottonwood tree and came to a stop. A cloud of dust lingered in the morning air as he turned the engine off, opened his door, and stepped out. "Grab your stuff, son," he said. "Let's not keep the fish waiting."

Jacob and William collected their fishing gear from the back seat of the family car. Jacob then led the way as they shuffled off towards the river. Reaching the bank, he turned to William and announced, "I'm heading upstream a bit. There's a nice hole just below that point up there."

"Okay, Dad," William replied, "I'm going to try around the bridge here."

"There's some pretty snaggy rocks," Jacob informed him. "If you're going to use a spinner, you'd better make it a small one."

"Okay Dad, thanks," William replied as Jacob paced off towards the gravel point some sixty yards or so upstream. William set his tackle box down and slipped together the two pieces of his fishing pole. Making sure that they were positioned correctly, he fed line from the reel and threaded it through the eyelets. He then opened his tackle box and retrieved a snap-swivel. After he tied it to the line, he searched through the tackle box for just the right lure. Noticing that the water was fairly cloudy, he selected a small yellow and green spinner with a bright silver blade. *Yeah, that'll do,* he thought.

On his fourth cast, William got his first strike. However, he tried to set the hook too quickly and missed the opportunity. Noting the spot where he'd felt the strike, he made his next cast about eight feet beyond it and began slowly reeling in the line. When he again felt a light strike on the lure, he let it settle for about half a second before beginning to bump it back in once more in a start and stop fashion.

One more light strike was followed by a jolt so strong and sudden that it nearly pulled the pole from his hand! He yanked on the pole, setting the hook deeply. There was a loud zinging sound as line stripped from the reel. "Fish on!" he hollered in gleeful enthusiasm. Twitching his pole this way and that, William did what he could to steer his prey clear of partially submerged brush and other potential entanglements, where it was attempting to find sanctuary. "No you don't! Get back here!" William chided, as he paced up and down the bank of the river, taking up line whenever he could. He was about to holler for his dad to bring the net, but as he turned upstream, he noticed that he was busy with a fish of his own. *Nuts!* he thought. *I'll have to let him get real tired out, I guess.*

After a couple more minutes of playing the fish out, William turned upstream again to see his dad walking towards him with the net. Jacob called out, "Hey there, son... what ya' got on the line?"

"I think it's a trout," William replied, "but I haven't got him in close enough to see yet. He's a beast!"

Just then, William's line took off upstream; slicing through the water. Tiny droplets sprang from the line as it pulled taut, threatening to break. Through the cloudy stream, Jacob caught a quick glance at the fish as it turned broadside to the shore. "Wow! He *is* huge! Don't you dare lose him, boy. Keep playing him out and let him get tired. I'll net him when he gets close enough."

Jacob waded out into the chilly water until it had climbed half way up his shins. William played the fish back in his direction as he tensely waited. When the fish swam close enough, Jacob lunged out with the net. "Dang! Missed him," he apologetically announced. "Bring him around again." Now aware of Jacob's proximity, the fish swung wide and took off upstream, heading for the submerged brush again. "Ho there!" Jacob shouted, "keep him out of that brush, boy!"

"Yeah, yeah… I know," William replied, "he tried that before."

The next time that William got the fish within striking distance of the net, Jacob managed to land him. "Great fish!" he exclaimed, as he waded back to shore. Lifting it by one of its gill plates, he held the fish up for William to see.

William's eyes ogled the eighteen-inch long monster. It looked somewhat like a very large cutthroat trout, but had a yellow head with black spots. A band along the top of its back was a light metallic blue color and its fins were yellowish-orange. "What kind of a trout is *that*?" he asked.

"That's a *Gila* trout," Jacob replied, "an Arizona native. It's a real lunker, too. That's just about as big as they get. Great catch, son!"

Somewhat confused, William asked, "Gila? …like that weird lizard thing?"

"No… that's different," Jacob replied, somewhat amused at his son's confused inquiry.

William took the fish from his dad and threaded it onto his stringer. He then tied the opposite end off to a large tree branch that lay along the riverbank before lowering the fish back into the chilly water. William smiled with a grim satisfaction as the trout immediately made a break for the open water, only to discover the limiting factor of the stringer. "Fat chance!" William taunted.

Over the next few hours, William caught several more fish. Three more trout were added to his stringer, as well as two small-mouth bass. Changing his line over to a hook and bobber setup, he then walked downstream to a deep, calm stretch of river. He diced several small cubes from a hot dog he'd retrieved from the cooler and ended up adding three large crappie to his stringer as well.

Jacob finished the expedition with two trout and three catfish. When the fishing began to slow down in the early afternoon, they decided to pack up and head home for a late lunch. The pain of the stringer cutting into his hand as he returned to the car delighted William to no end. *I can't believe I out-fished Dad*, he thought.

As they pulled up to the house, William slyly began, "It's still uh... loser cleans the fish, right?"

"Just itching for the belt, aren't we?" Jacob jokingly replied, as he stepped out of the car. "Put your stuff away, Mister Smarty. I'll take care of the fish."

William triumphantly stowed his pole and tackle box back in his room before heading out to the kitchen. As he made himself a couple of sandwiches, he shared every detail of the day with his grandma and his sister Leslie, who was planning to leave for home early the next morning. Jacob, who was cleaning the fish in the utility room sink, pretended not to hear.

When William had finished eating lunch, he returned to his room to grab his new b.b. gun. He couldn't wait to try it out. As he made his way back through the house, his mom spotted him as she carried a laundry basket down the stairs. "Hey there, buckaroo!" she said. "Are you off to murder some soup cans?"

"Yeah, I thought I'd squeeze in a little mayhem before dinner," William quipped. "Say, if you really want to make Dad's day, ask him how the fishing trip went."

Theresa caught the hint. "Oh, really?" she grinned. "I'll do that."

As William passed through the utility room, he stopped to check on his dad's progress with the fish. Jacob set the task aside for a moment to make sure that his son knew how to safely use the b.b. gun. "That's the business end," he said. "Always be aware of where it's pointed, even if you don't think that there's any b.b.s left in it."

Before he went outside, William retrieved a small wooden crate from the back corner of the room. To his delight, there were several old cans sitting inside of it. He carried the crate with him as he walked outside and across the back lawn to the far end of the house.

He set the b.b. gun down as he paced over to a tree that stood near the edge of the lawn and dumped the cans out of the crate. After placing the crate upside-down in front of the tree, he set the cans up on it before returning to where the b.b. gun lay near the garden shed. A small canister of ammunition had come with the b.b. gun. Withdrawing this from his pocket, he filled the air rifle with copper spheres until it wouldn't hold any more. He then pumped the handle as many times as he could, before taking aim at the stack of cans. He took a deep breath, holding it as he sighted down the barrel, across the lawn, and to the "O" on the label of a family-sized soup can. Squinting one eye, he prepared for the moment of victory.

"Hey, what's up Billy?" Sharon Stewart interrupted him. "I hear you had a birthday, or something." She approached from his left, rounding the corner of the house and pacing across the lawn, casually gazing at can-covered crate.

Still taking aim at the cans, William experienced a brief flash of evil intent. *No, no, William... he thought, you'd never live to see thirteen!* The brief flash of sadistic anger was quickly replaced by a sudden twinge of conscience. Despite the sting of her chiding, William was aware that he hadn't exactly been neighborly to her, either. This new feeling caught him somewhat off guard. Somehow, something was different inside of him now.

"Hi ya', Shari-Pie," he said, in a deliberately inoffensive tone. "Yeah, it was yesterday. I would have invited you... but we went out of town." He squeezed off his first shot, just missing one of the cans.

"No problem," Sharon replied, "I was shopping with my mom all day. We stopped for pizza on the way home."

William paused, leaning the b.b. gun against the garden shed. He then turned towards Sharon and shyly began, "Um, I'm... well... sorry for not being so nice to you before." Sharon blushed slightly and looked aside as William continued. "It's just that, well, I've never had to move to a new place before. And it's been really hard leaving all of my friends behind."

"Yeah, well... I was kind of a little mean spirited too," Sharon confessed. "I just get a little *disturbed* when people make fun of my hair. And besides," she playfully glared, "you did heave a rock at me!" After a moment of silence, she extended a pinkie. "Truce?" she offered.

William momentarily clasp her extended pinkie with his own. "Truce!" he agreed. "You know," he then began, "my mom's got red hair too. She'd kill me outright if she ever found out that I'd made fun of a red-head."

"Like my dad says," Sharon replied, "Forgiven means forgotten. I've gotta' get going now," she continued. "See you later, Silly-Billy!"

William waved goodbye before turning to retrieve his b.b. gun. A small light had gone on inside of him. He was, indeed, somehow different now.

Chapter
Nineteen

William's alarm clock woke him at five-thirty the next morning. Although he usually didn't set his alarm during summer vacation, this was one of those special occasions when he had. He wanted to be sure to be up early enough to see his sister Leslie off as she returned home to Los Angeles.

Awkward, sleepy fingers required nearly half a minute to locate and turn off the alarm. William yawned and shook his head, his face contorting into what would, under other circumstances, have been a terrifying grimace. He then wrinkled his brow, stretching his eyes open as far as they would go. Another yawn, and he slid his legs out from under the covers and stood up.

After completing his daily business in the bathroom, he returned to his bedroom and got dressed. Planning on returning to the Ankara village later that day, he set aside the new clothes he'd received for his birthday and slid on an older pair of jeans and a t-shirt instead. Although he was usually pretty casual in his choice of attire, dressing in whatever his fingers found first, he knew that his mother would have a fit if he headed out to the cave in his brand new clothes. He knew that she would want them saved for school and church.

After he finished getting dressed, William paced off to the kitchen, where Mary was busy cooking an early breakfast for Leslie. "Good morning, Grandma," he greeted Mary as he entered the kitchen. "Is Leslie up yet?"

"She'll be back any second," Mary replied. "She just took her suitcase out to the car. You want some breakfast while I'm at it?"

"Um, no thanks," William replied. "I'm not that hungry just yet. I'll make some toast or something after I collect the eggs."

Mary finished preparing Leslie's breakfast and carried it out to the dining room table, just as Leslie returned. "Thanks, Granny!" she said. "You're terrific." Then, turning to William, she said, "Good morning, little spud!"

"Hey there, slug!" William replied. "You taking off soon?"

As Leslie took a seat and began eating, she replied, "Yep, as soon as I finish eating. Of course, I've gotta' say goodbye to Mom and Dad first."

"Have you decided which way you're heading home yet?" William inquired. "Are you heading north or south?"

"Well," Leslie replied, "I was really into the idea of heading south and taking a little detour to see Tombstone, but that'd just put me too far out of the way. I'd have to drive a good part of the night to make up the time. So, I'll just head north and swing by the Grand Canyon on the way back. Maybe the next time I'm out this way, you and I can head down and spend the day at Tombstone."

"That'd be great," William replied. "I hear they've got some pretty cool old-west shows there... gunfights in the street and everything!"

"Well, Dad told me last night that he was taking you camping somewhere?" Leslie inquired.

"Yeah, in a couple of weeks," William replied. "He said it's someplace he used to go west of here, in the White Mountains."

As William and Leslie talked, the aroma of coffee brewing made its way from the kitchen counter, through the dining room, and into the front room of the house. It then slithered up the stairs and into Jacob and Theresa's bedroom. Stirring from a sound sleep, Jacob stretched and sat up. Then, hearing the faint voices from downstairs, he reached over and shook his wife's shoulder. "Wake up, honey. It sounds like Leslie's getting ready to take off."

Leslie had just finished her breakfast as Jacob and Theresa came plodding down the stairs. "Good morning, sweetie," Theresa began, sleepily. "Are you running out on us?"

"Yeah, I think I've got everything together," Leslie replied. "I love you guys. I'll try to make it back again around the holidays."

The family made their way out to the front lawn, saying their goodbyes as Leslie slid behind the steering wheel of her car. As she pulled away waving, they lingered for several moments, watching as a cloud of dust pursued her into the distance. As the car crested a small rise in the road, disappearing over the far side, they turned again to the house.

After William collected the eggs, he made himself breakfast. When he'd finished eating and setting his dishes in the sink, he returned to his room. Pulling his backpack from the closet, he searched his belongings for some sort of a gift that he could take with him to the Ankara village.

Considering a number of options, he finally settled on an old set of Lincoln Logs. *They can build all kinds of neat stuff with these,* he thought as he stuffed them into his backpack. He then spied a set of Pick-Up Sticks and put them in as well. Lastly, he added a few small toys cars to the backpack, thinking that the Ankara children might enjoy playing with them.

Satisfied, he picked the backpack up and headed for the kitchen. Searching through the refrigerator, he selected an apple and a few carrots. He stuffed these into his backpack, in case he got hungry before returning home for lunch. Remembering that he had left his bike in front of the house the last time he'd ridden it, he went outside by way of the front door.

Strapping on his backpack, William mounted his bike and took off towards the familiar trail that led out to the cave. The morning was clear and unusually crisp for early August. A few high, feathery clouds graced a sky that was otherwise as blue as the Caribbean. Scores of grasshoppers leapt out of the path of William's bike as he peddled across the pasture. Several of these took flight upon leaping into the air. *Grasshoppers got wings already,* he thought. *Fall must be coming real early this year.*

After making his way across the pasture and over the distant hill, William parked his bike a short distance from the cave. He paced over to the opening and made his way down the slope. Walking over to the far left corner of the cave, he pulled the couch forward a few inches and slid his makeshift wall out of the way of the opening that led to the Ankara village.

As he did, a distant sound caught his ear. *They're singing again,* he thought. *They sure do sing a lot.* As William stood there listening for a moment, he noticed that there was something different in the tone of the music than what he'd heard before. Although they sang in their native language and the voices were quite distant, William could still hear... no, *feel* something very distinctive in the song. There was... a sadness to it. And a sense of desperation.

Retrieving his rope from where he'd tossed it aside before, he tied it off to one of the heavy wooden legs of the couch. He then gathered the rest of the rope into a loose bundle and tossed it through the opening in the cave wall.

After dropping his backpack through as well, he climbed up onto the back of the couch and took hold of the rope. Swinging first one leg through the opening and then the other, he cautiously lowered himself down into the darkness.

Locating his backpack by touch, he unzipped it and inserted a hand. *There it is,* he thought, locating the towel that he'd wrapped his flashlight in to pad it. Unwrapping the towel, he retrieved the flashlight and flicked it on. It shone brightly for a second or two, before languishing to a deep amber. It then extinguished completely. William then realized that he'd never gotten around to changing the batteries after his first trip to the village.

Pausing for several minutes, he considered his options. Remembering the candles stored in the fort, he climbed back up the rope and retrieved several, along with a dozen or so matches. He stuffed these into his pocket and climbed slowly back down into the depths again.

He then retrieved a candle and a match from his pocket. He struck the wooden match on the wall of the cave and it flared to life. Tipping the match sideways, he lit the candle before discarding the used match. As the flame grew to its full strength, he held it high in the air and looked around. The cavern looked quite different than it had when it was flooded by the pure radiance of Sador's Shekinah stone. It now looked... well... creepy.

Catching his bearings, William retrieved his backpack and carefully stepped off towards the passageway that led to the Ankara village. The strange, mournful song had grown to a crescendo a few moments before and was now gradually fading away. Although he had no cognitive understanding of what was being expressed, William again noted the sadness and the pleading tone in the voices. *I wonder... what's wrong?* As he drew closer to the village, the light from the Pool Of Truth grew bright enough that he no longer needed the candle. He blew it out and returned it to his pocket after it had cooled. He then continued on.

As he slowly entered the village, one set of eyes after another rose to meet his gaze, only to turn away again in anger, or grief, or a strange mixture of both. "Young lord!" a voice called out from his left. William turned to see Sador standing outside of one of the Ankara homes. As he looked closer, he noticed Lucinda standing just inside the door and realized that this must be the home of his friend, Enid.

"Hello, Sador," he replied. Then, slightly shifting his gaze to Lucinda, he asked, "Where's Enid? I brought some gifts for you guys."

Lucinda's sparsely buried grief overflowed. Sobbing openly, she retreated into the house. Now, both embarrassed and frightened, William pled, "What? What's wrong? Where's Enid?"

Sador stepped forward slightly, as if attempting to shelter Lucinda from William's unintentional assault. "Young lord," he began, "walk with me…" He motioned towards the Pool Of Truth and began walking. William followed. As they reached the shining water's edge, Sador came to a stop, gazing into the radiant depths. The silence grew very uncomfortable for William.

"Um, Sador?" he cautiously began.

"Young lord," Sador interrupted, "Enid, your friend… and my son, lies gravely injured. He may not live."

"What?!?" William exploded! "What do you mean? How?" Both grief and anger overtook him at once.

"Marshok…" Sador winced as he bit out the name, "Marshok led a band of the dark ones back to this village a few nights ago, while most of our gatherers were out collecting food. On all previous raids, it had for the most part been our sound stones and fire stones that they were after. And so, we had several guards assigned to protect our remaining supply. However, the dark ones overpowered the guards, killing two of them. They managed to steal most of the stones before reinforcements arrived."

William's anger grew as Sador looked up at him and continued. "Enid, along with two others, secretly followed at a distance as the dark ones fled. At one point, when they assumed that they were safely away, the dark ones stopped to rest. Enid crept close enough to overhear their discussion. He apparently discovered the dark scheme behind these raids."

William's eyes grew wide. "What?" he asked. "What's that?"

Sador sighed, looking into the shining waters again. "We do not know, young lord. As Enid rose from his hiding place in order to rejoin the others and return to the village, he was spotted. One of the dark one's arrows struck him in the arm as he fled."

"In the arm?" William asked, slightly confused.

"Remember, young lord," Sador began, "the dark ones lace their weapons with poison. However, the arrow that struck Enid was fired in haste. If the poison had been freshly applied, Enid would not be alive."

"He's… okay then?" William asked.

"He lies gravely wounded," Sador replied. "Lucinda has done all that she can for him, but his recovery is uncertain." Choking back tears, he continued, "He is delirious with fever, speaking only of *the great deluge*… and a dark plan. The others who were with him do not know of what he speaks. He fell unconscious before he could tell them what he'd overheard."

"But, can't you just bring him here and give him some of this water of yours?" William asked.

"The healing properties of this water," Sador began slowly, "only work if it is ingested of one's conscious choice and free will. It cannot be imposed. Enid is presently too ill… too delirious… to make this choice of his own free will."

William's grief and worry flared once again into a vindictive anger. "I've got a bunch of fireworks left over from the Fourth of July ! Find out where those creeps hang out, and I'll blow them to pieces!'

Shock and disgust covered Sador's face as he turned again to face William. "No! Do not speak of such vile things in my presence! How dare you!"

Somewhat taken aback, William protested, "What?"

"There is still much darkness in your own heart," Sador flatly replied. "You would use an act of darkness... to fight darkness?" he asked, pointedly. "Look around you," Sador continued, "As it is in the material world, so it is in the spiritual. It is *light* that dispels darkness. An evil act would only propagate more evil."

"It's not evil to defend yourself!" William hotly retorted.

Now somewhat enraged himself, Sador clenched his fists. After taking a moment to calm himself, he turned and spoke slowly and matter-of-factly to William. "Although they have done this vile thing," he began, "the dark ones... are still our brothers. They have been deceived and taken captive by the powers of Hell and the passions of the flesh, which they now serve. Remember young lord, the dark stain of sin found its origin in *your race.* They are victims as much as they are villains. Although in their present state, not one of them would shed a single tear over our demise, we wish them no harm. We daily pray that they may someday... somehow... return to the light of truth."

There was a definite note of finality in Sador's voice. "You... should go now," he said. "Our village is heavy with grief. If you wish, you may return tomorrow. We may know by then if Enid will survive."

William said not another word. He turned and slowly made his way back through the village. Just as he was about to enter the long passageway leading to the outer room, he paused. Removing the gifts he'd brought from his backpack, he set them down on the ground before continuing on. it seemed somewhat of a trivial act at this point, but perhaps these things would be of some use.

Vigil

A quiet spirit
searches the dawn
in earnest, fervent desire;
probing…
pleading…
drawn to the sacred source
as moths are drawn to fire.

A tiny spark
so frail and dim
scans the sky anew;
listening…
longing…
seeking the flame
from which it flew.

Michael M. Middleton

from Sacred Journeys
Copyright 2002

Chapter
Twenty

A joyless bike ride home followed William's exit from the cave. he spent most of the remainder of the day in his room before settling into a restless sleep that night. Anger, fear, and grief all vied for his soul as he slept.

At one point, he found himself suddenly wide-awake, his tear-streaked face bathed in the silvery-white glow of a full moon. It reminded him of the brilliant sheen that emanated from the Pool of Truth and he felt, for a moment, unsure of where he was. But then the memories of the day returned to trouble his young mind once again. A fiery grief rose up within him. Its weight rested heavy upon his heart and he found himself sobbing in shallow, staccato gasps.

After a time, he fell asleep once more, only to awaken again a short time later. Most of the night passed in this manner. After several failed attempts at sleeping through the remainder of the night, he finally abandoned the effort as the first faint traces of dawn crept over the far horizon.

Sleepily, he got dressed and quietly made his way through the house and out to the back porch. Slipping on his boots, he paced across the back lawn to a bench, which sat facing the dawn. Many troubling thoughts and questions plagued his young mind, obscuring his appreciation of the beauty before him. Bathed in the first light of a new day, he prayed for his friend Enid and the rest of the Ankara.

After completing his chores and making an attempt at eating breakfast, William let his parents know that he was heading back out to the cave. Several times, he answered, "I'm fine!" or "…just a little sleepy," to their concerned inquiries.

"You seem kinda' down," his grandmother observed. "Are you feeling okay, boy?" she asked.

"I'm fine…" he said one last time, as he strapped on his backpack and mounted his bike. "I, uh… might be a little late for lunch… I don't know."

"Well, I'm making a pot of turkey-noodle soup," Mary replied as he peddled across the yard. "I'll leave what's left sitting on the stove for ya'. Just help yourself when you get back."

Half of William wanted to get out to the cave as quickly as he could. The other half, however, feared what he might find and wanted to take its time. More than once, fear gained the upper hand and he almost turned back. However, compassion and courage won out in the end and William was soon making his way through the underground world on his way to the Ankara village.

An uncharacteristic silence filled the air as he caught his first distant glimpse of the village. This strange quiet disturbed him, but he continued on nevertheless. As he entered the village, he observed a great throng of Ankara surrounding the Pool of Truth, some distance from its edge. William watched from a distance as the mass of small gray creatures parted and a solitary figure made his way through the assembly to the water's edge.

As the creature painfully bent to drink, William concluded that it must be Enid. *He's alright!* he thought. *He made it!* Joy and relief blazed anew within William as the revitalized creature stood, looking back in his direction. Though the distance was too great to clearly see such a small being, something in his stature told William that it was indeed his friend.

A warm greeting was cut short by the concerned and somber tone of Enid's voice as William approached. "William, it is good to see you. However, I am grieved that it is under such dire circumstances that we meet again."

"What is it?" William asked. "What's Marshok up to? What did you hear?"

Sador stepped forward. "I am afraid," he began, "that many of your race are in grave danger; a danger that they can neither foresee nor prevent."

William's eyes grew wide. Again turning to Enid, he pointedly asked, "What is it? What did you hear?"

"The dark ones," Enid began, "have stolen a great number of sound stones and fire stones... not just from our village, but from others as well."

"And...?" William pressed.

Enid continued, "I overheard them speaking of using the stones... to destroy the structures that your race has built in order to restrain the mighty rivers."

"Blow up dams?" William asked, incredulously. "With little rocks? I don't get it. There's a lot of dams around here, but what can little rocks do to a great big dam?"

"You forget the *nature* of these particular stones!" Sador interrupted. "The sound stones greatly amplify *any vibration*. Dams generate a lot of vibration, young lord."

Enid spoke again. "From what I overheard of the dark one's conversation, they plan on placing numerous sound stones within channels they have excavated underneath and around the dams. The normal vibrations of the falling water would then be amplified many thousands of times in a chain reaction, causing a catastrophic failure of the dam... and great loss of life from the resulting deluge."

"And the fire stones," Sador added, "if placed strategically, would generate a great deal of heat, rapidly accelerating the process."

The plausibility of this concept gradually became real to William. A cold chill shot up his spine as he asked, "Which one? Where are they planning on doing this? I mean, there's *a lot* of dams around here... Horseshoe Dam, Bartlette Dam, Mormon Flat, Hoover... Where are they planning on doing this?"

"That, I do not know," answered Enid.

"You don't know?!?" William snipped. "You've gotta' know! Thousands and thousands of people could die! We've gotta' do something!"

Staring him square in the eye, Enid flatly replied, "I do not know, William."

There was a tense, desperate silence, until Sador spoke again. "William, we have sent out additional scouts to try and locate where the dark ones are hiding as they prepare to strike. Perhaps, when they return, we will know more. But..." he trailed off.

"But, what?" asked William, noting the hesitancy in Sador's voice. "You *are* going to stop them, aren't you?"

Sador, with a note of sorrowful resignation in his voice, replied, "Yes, young lord... stop them we must. But the means by which we *may*... this is troubling to me. It is not within our nature to cause harm. And yet, if we remain true to this instinct, even to the point of allowing the dark ones to succeed in their vile scheme, shall not a greater guilt be ascribed to us?" Sador paused briefly, as his eyes scanned the Ankara village. His gaze then returned once again to meet William's "We have never had to face this terrible question before, young friend. Is it acceptable, when absolutely necessary, to cause harm in order to prevent a greater harm?"

A tormented silence filled the great cavern as this burning question rang within every heart and mind. William was about to speak, when he was suddenly cut short by a long trumpet blast, followed by numerous shorter tones. "The scouts!" Enid announced. "They have returned!"

Chapter
Twenty-One

In the distance, a small band of Ankara came into view. They entered the great cavern through a small fissure in the far wall, some sixty feet or so beyond the edge of the village. As they strode forward, their forms illumined by the overflowing radiance from the Pool of Truth, greatly relieved wives and children ran out to meet them. In the midst of this joyous reunion, one of the scouts spotted Sador standing next to William. As their eyes met, his expression changed from that of a childlike joy to one much more somber and urgent. Without breaking his hold on Sador's gaze, the scout made his way swiftly across the cavern, until he stood but a short distance away.

"We must talk," he began. "We have discovered the location of the dark ones' camp, as well as further details of their plan." William noted the urgency in his voice.

Sador paused briefly, and then simply replied, "Gather the council." William began to follow as Sador paced off across the cavern, but a stern look told him that he was not meant to do so. He watched from a distance as a dozen or so Ankara men and women removed their sound stone necklaces and filed into a comparatively large structure at one end of the village. They obviously intended to keep their discussion of this issue private.

After a torturous thirty or forty minute wait, William saw Sador and the others emerging from the building. Restraining his emotional impulse, William stayed put, waiting as Sador slowly approached. Slipping on his sound stone necklace, Sador looked up into William's eyes. Grief and concern etched deeply across his face, he began, "Young lord, we have come to a conclusion. We shall do... whatever is necessary, in order to stop the dark ones' scheme."

Sador's obvious emotional turmoil dampened William's lust for revenge. Now somewhat ashamed of his impetuous desire to exact punishment upon the dark ones, he meekly asked, "What can I do? I can help, if..."

"You may remain here," Sador interrupted, "and help to protect the village, should the dark ones return. You are... too large to follow where we must go."

William agreed to stand guard over the village, grateful that he could at least help in some way. Taking a seat against the wall of the cave, he watched in fascination as an army assembled before him. Over the course of twenty minutes or so, nearly every adult male in the village gathered around Sador.

Many of them wore makeshift armor, fashioned out of empty walnut shells and a number of other natural materials. A few brandished metal shields, which looked as if they had once been soup-can lids. Remembering the melted spring of the mousetrap, he concluded that the Ankara must actually, in some measure, be able to craft metal using the fire stones. This assumption found reinforcement, as William noted another villager approaching, clad in a shiny metal breastplate.

Most of the soldiers carried a weapon of some sort, either a spear or a bow. But as William looked closer, he noted that many carried only a coil of rope or a net draped neatly over one shoulder. And still others carried only Shekinah stones. As Sador gave instruction, they formed into ranks. Those carrying the Shekinah stones assembled in front, followed by those carrying the ropes and nets. Finally, those carrying offensive weapons took up the rear.

Breaking his silence, William leaned forward and called out to Sador, "Um, I think you've got that backwards. Shouldn't the guys with the spears and stuff be in the front?"

Sador coldly replied, "Though we are willing, *if absolutely necessary*, to inflict injury... it is not our desire to do so. We shall first confront our fallen brothers with the light of truth from the Great Book. Our hope is that many shall find the courage and resolve to return to the fellowship of the true path. We shall attempt to take captive those who will not, at least until we can recover all of the fire stones and sound stones."

"You're kidding, right?" William asked. "Those unarmed guys in front are gonna' get slaughtered!"

"Do not presume to instruct us in warfare," Sador replied. "Unlike those of your race," he said coldly, "we value the lives of our fallen brothers as much as we value our own lives. And besides," he continued, "they do carry Shekinah stones. As you have experienced for yourself, the light of truth can be quite devastating to one who walks in darkness."

Feeling rather diminished, William sunk back against the wall of the cave, saying not another word. He watched in silence as Sador led the assembled throng across the great cavern, disappearing through the fissure in the far wall. He failed, however, to notice Lucinda secretly following them at a distance.

Chapter
Twenty-Two

Picking their way through the deep and secret places of the earth, the reluctant army cautiously made their way to the dark ones' camp. As those in the lead first caught sight of the camp, they suddenly halted. Hiding themselves behind scattered boulders, they knelt in silent prayer.

In the distance, several dozen of the dark ones huddled around tiny campfires. Some were eating, while others appeared to be tending to their weapons. A few were brewing fresh batches of the poison that would later be applied to their spears and arrows. Its rancid, acrid odor filled the air. The stolen sound stones and fire stones lay in two large piles, surrounded by numerous sentries. Fortunately, these sentries had failed to notice the approach of Sador and the others.

Enid was placed in charge of the soldiers who carried offensive weapons. They quietly fanned out, positioning themselves so as to prevent the escape of those who would try to flee. This took a good deal of time, as a number of fissures and passageways led off in many directions.

When all was set, Sador raised a tiny trumpet, crafted from a snail shell. Inhaling deeply, he pressed it to his lips and blew. A sound stone mounted within the shell produced a clear, vibrant tone, which resonated throughout the cavern.

Shock and terror suddenly filled the hearts of the dark ones, as dozens of Shekinah stones flamed to life at once. The Ankara who held them aloft began to advance on the encampment. As they did, they sang holy songs of truth from the Great Book. As their voices thundered throughout the deep places of the earth, the light of revelation blazed like a billion newborn suns, swallowing the darkness.

Enraged and terrified, several of the dark ones blindly launched arrows and spears into the shining void. Only one found its mark, striking Sador in the shoulder. Enid, seeing him fall, ran to him. "Father!" he cried. "Father!"

Sador sat up, bracing himself against a large stone. "I... will be okay," he said, "the wound is not deep." The unspoken question burned within Enid's heart, clearly expressing itself in his eyes. Noting this concern, Sador pulled the arrow from his flesh with a quick jerk. Examining the tip, he noted, "It is clean, my son. It carried no poison."

Several of the dark ones fled, carrying a few of the sound stones and fire stones away with them. But most of them were subdued and taken captive by the Ankara from the village. A very few of the dark ones still carried a faint memory of the fellowship of the light and surrendered willingly.

Attempting to flee through a passageway that the others hadn't yet noticed, Marshok suddenly found his way blocked by a shadowy figure. Reflexively, he raised his spear; its tip dripping with freshly applied poison. He was about to strike, when Lucinda stepped forward into the light.

A burning grief rapidly quenched the rage in his dark heart. The rage then asserted itself once again, clouding his mind and clawing at his soul. Marshok found himself violently torn by opposing impulses. The titanic struggle within drove him to the brink of madness.

Finally overcome by grief and shame, he dropped his spear and turned to flee in the opposite direction. However, he found his retreat blocked by several of the Ankara soldiers. As one of them raised a spear, preparing to strike, a hideous, cold fear swept over Marshok. Lucinda finally spoke, "Hold! Do not harm him, he has dropped his weapon."

Enid stood amongst this particular group of soldiers. As he heard his wife's voice, he cried out, "Lucinda! Why are you here? Are you harmed?" Fear was evident in his voice, as well as a note of anger.

"I am unharmed," she replied.

Refocusing his gaze onto Marshok, Enid seemed to sense the battle that raged within him. First laying aside his own impure impulses, Enid spoke in a firm yet gentle tone. "Marshok... Brother... All is forgiven, if you will but return to the fellowship of the light. Forsake the ways of darkness and you shall be fully restored."

The tiny, cold ember of goodness and truth, which had lain dormant within Marshok suddenly ignited. He did not receive full healing in this one instant, but he did lay hold of the courage to admit his need. Collapsing onto the cold, damp floor of the cave, he sobbed, "I'm sorry... I'm so sorry!"

<u>Choice</u>

What wonders await
the wayward one
when they finally turn;
what joy will fill
the bleakest heart
when they finally learn
that grace is free
and freely flows
to any heart which yearns.

Michael M. Middleton

from Modern Musings
Copyright 2003

Chapter
Twenty-Three

Applying a poultice to Sador's wounded shoulder, Lucinda then dressed it with a clean strip of cloth taken from the small pouch of medicinal supplies that she carried on her hip. "This should stop the bleeding and ease the pain," she said, "until we have returned to the village and the healing waters of the pool." Marshok, having composed himself somewhat, helped Sador to his feet. Every eye looked to Sador, awaiting his instruction.

Enid and several others were given the task of escorting those who'd been taken captive back to the village. The prisoners' hands were lashed behind their backs and a rope tied around their waists secured them together in groups of a half-dozen or so. Igniting a Shekinah stone to light the way, Enid set off, leading the unhappy band back to the Ankara village.

Ashamedly averting his eyes as they departed, Marshok's heart was nearly crushed by the overwhelming weight of guilt and regret. "That... That should be me," he said. "I was their leader... and the architect of this dark scheme."

"But you have turned from the dark path," Sador replied. "Forgiveness is yours now. And full healing will come in due course, providing that you lay hold of the courage to pay the price required by the Pool of Truth."

Marshok winced at this thought. "Sador," he began, "my guilt runs deeper than you know." Sensing a deepening anguish, Sador remained still and silent, observing Marshok's frame through compassionate eyes. "The men... those who were killed in that last raid," he continued, "it was by my hand."

For a long time, Sador said nothing. Finally laying hold of sufficient inner strength to cope with this revelation, he gently placed a hand on Marshok's shoulder. "That is a heavy burden to bear, my son," he said. "The path to restoration shall not be an easy one. But it begins now."

Lucinda and the others from the village who'd stayed behind to collect the stolen sound stones and fire stones waited a short distance away. The dark ones who'd willingly surrendered waited there as well, assisting in this task. Motioning in their direction, Sador led off, beginning the long trek back to the village. Each hesitant step purchased a minute degree of renewed courage as Marshok followed.

As Sador and the others arrived back at the village, William was there to greet them. Sador made his way directly to William, knowing that he would have many questions. "Greetings, young lord!" he called out. Thank you for watching over the village in my absence."

"Is everything alright?" William asked. "I saw Enid come back with the prisoners, but he wouldn't tell me anything."

"It has been a difficult day," Sador replied. "...But a good one." he then added. "We have accomplished our task, and with no loss of life on either side."

"You're kidding!" William replied. "That's so cool!" A measure of hesitancy revealed itself in Sador's eyes. Sensing that something wasn't quite right, William then asked, "Um, what is it? Is something wrong?"

Sador replied, "A few of the dark ones eluded us, young lord. They carried some of the stones away as they fled, and may still attempt to carry out their plan in some measure." A few moments of silence passed as William contemplated the reality of this continuing threat. "But," Sador then continued, "several of our fallen brothers have repented of their dark ways. Even Marshok himself has returned to us in peace."

"Marshok?" William asked. "Really? That's terrific!"

"Yes it is," Sador replied. "But a very difficult path lies ahead for Marshok and the others. In order to find true healing, they must fully embrace the revelation which comes from the Pool of Truth." Pausing as he gazed deeply into William's eyes, he continued, "There is a real danger in this, young lord. It is uncertain whether or not they will be able to find the courage and resolve within themselves to survive this encounter. Conviction and condemnation can easily be confused. Conviction, if rightly received and acted upon, is the first step on the path to healing and restoration. However, if one falters and allows truth to become *condemnation* instead, they are in mortal danger of returning to the ways of darkness."

Digesting Sador's words to the fullest measure that he could, William then changed the subject a bit. "So... what are you going to do with the bad guys that Enid brought back?"

For the first time, William noted an empty look in Sador's eyes. "I do not know, William. We must... detain them for a time," he replied, "for the common good. Perhaps, some of them may return to the fellowship. If not, I do not know what shall be done."

William headed home late that afternoon. A strange mixture of joy and sorrow… relief and worry… filled his mind and heart. He was tremendously relieved that the dark ones' plan had been averted and that his friends had safely returned. However, he recalled Sador's warning that those who had escaped could still be a threat. This concern would plague his thoughts and haunt his dreams for many years to come.

After a time, Marshok and the others who'd returned to the fellowship of the light found the courage to partake of the Pool of Truth. Determined to make restitution for their past deeds, many of them then set out to carry the message of restoration to the dark ones who'd escaped on that day. Over the following decades, they would secretly traverse Adam's domain, seeking out all those of their race whose hearts had been taken captive by the ways of darkness. They did all that they could to share the words of truth and healing from the Great Book, waiting upon the restoration of all things that the Lord of lords would one day bring to pass.

"He who covers his sins
will not prosper,
But whoever confesses and
forsakes them will have mercy."
Proverbs 28:13, NKJV

"'Come now and let us reason together,'
Says the LORD,
'Though your sins are like scarlet,
They shall be as white as snow;
Though they are red like crimson,
They shall be as wool.'"
Isaiah 1:18, NKJV

"If we say that we have fellowship with Him,
and walk in darkness, we lie and do not practice the
truth. But if we walk in the light as He is in the light,
we have fellowship with one another,
and the blood of Jesus Christ His Son cleanses us from all sin."
1 John 1:6-7, NKJV

Bubbles on the Grass

Like bubbles on the grass,
childhood must pass;
the mockery of time
will claim its prize at last.

Carefree summer days,
kissed by golden rays,
fade from fact,
to fancy…
to melancholy haze.

The light of life dies dim
and summer joys grow grim;
the flower of youth falls faint,
as leaves fall from the limb.

Yet will come a golden morn'
when the shroud of grief is torn
and winter's gray
is put away
and summer is reborn.

Michael M. Middleton

from Modern Musings
Copyright 2003

Chapter
Twenty-Four

Summer vacation had soon come to an end and William entered the sixth grade. Being the new kid in school wasn't nearly as bad as he had thought it would be. He quickly made a number of new friends and discovered an affinity for basketball. He did well in tryouts, easily qualifying as a first-string player. He also joined the school marching band the following spring and enjoyed a number of other extracurricular activities throughout his teen years.

By the time he'd begun his sophomore year of high school, he was fairly convinced of what he wanted to do with his life. The big-city boy from Reno had taken a liking to living in the country. He enrolled in every agriculture related class he could in school and participated in 4-H on a year-round basis. He eventually built a much larger chicken coop, expanding his egg business considerably. He even became a minor supplier to a couple of small grocery stores on the outskirts of Phoenix.

William learned everything that he could about horses from his grandmother Mary and took a few business courses through a community college after he'd completed high school. In addition to his egg business, he then invested in a few thoroughbred horses, attempting to re-ignite the embers of the traditional family business.

However, times had changed and this endeavor didn't pan out as well as he'd hoped. As his sister Leslie had done with her dreams of modeling, he then settled for the next best thing. With the blessing of his parents and grandmother, he incorporated the Thornton Family ranch as a western-style bed and breakfast. Riding instruction and guided horseback outings on the many scenic trails in the area were also offered. All of the vacant bedrooms in the house finally found a renewed purpose, as this business prospered greatly. After a few years, he even had to add additional accommodations to the property.

Although he hired on outside help to do the majority of the cooking, his grandmother's strawberry muffins remained a much-loved staple at breakfast. Nearly everyone who stayed at the ranch lavished magnanimous praise upon Mary's baking endeavors. Upon her death just three years prior to William taking a bride, his mother carried on the strawberry muffin tradition. To William's great surprise, she had become quite good at it.

Throughout the years, William continued to visit his friends in the Ankara village as frequently as his busy life would allow. When he was unable to make it to the village for a long spell, he would often leave out small, useful gifts for them on his windowsill or nightstand. The Ankara would leave behind a few pebbles or twigs as they collected the gifts, to let William know that they had been there and appreciated his generosity.

He also adopted his grandmother's tradition of reading from the Great Book early each morning as he sat at the small table by the kitchen window. When Mary had passed on, her picture was added to that of her dear husband Seth's in the family Bible. In later years, the portraits of William's mother and father would also be added to this place of honored remembrance.

Holding firm to the fires of revelation, William grew in knowledge and integrity throughout the passing years. All who associated with him could not help but know that he served someone greater than himself. Although his body eventually grew feeble and his mind diminished in focus, the radiance of life and truth within his spirit never dimmed. Holding fast to the words of truth, he continued in his fervent devotion to the Lord of lords as he awaited the Great Day.

<u>Growing Old</u>

The white upon my head,
the decaying of my teeth...
The comfort of my bed,
and the aching of my knees...
When all is done and said,
all these say to me...
"Good times lay ahead,
I'm closer yet to free!"

Michael M. Middleton

from Modern Musings
Copyright 2003

Chapter
Twenty-Five

In William's mind, the decades pass. Suddenly, the glint of headlights approaching down the dusty country lane captures his attention. As his grip on the glistening stone slackens, it dims, and his mind and spirit return to the present. He once again finds himself an old man, sitting on the porch. "Excuse me," he says to the fireflies, "but it looks like my sweet wife's home from the store." Stretching his legs, he once again grimaces at the number of 'cracks' that his ankle makes.

Rising from the handcrafted willow chair, he paces off towards the car as it comes to a stop. The boiling cloud of dust that lingers in the air causes him to cough repeatedly as he approaches. "Still drives like a maniac..." he mutters under his breath.

As the headlights extinguish, the driver's door opens. Out steps a slender woman of about William's age. A knowing look of mock disapproval spreads across her face as her gaze meets William's.

"What?" William asks, "What did I do?"

"You've been showing off for the fireflies again, haven't you?" the spry old lady asks.

Feigning innocence, William replies, "Who, me?"

Deftly brushing a lock of amber-streaked hair away from her face, she replies, "Yes, you! You lit up half the state!"

"Well, they started it!" he jests.

Handing William three small bags of groceries, she closes the car door and paces off towards the house. About half way to the porch, she looks back over her shoulder and chides, "Silly-Billy!"

Walking With God

To walk again in the cool of the day
through mist-shrouded gardens
beside crystal streams;
to stroll in sweet fellowship face to face
upon blossom-paved paths
with creation's King.

To walk once more upon the wind-swept shores
beside the Galilee
gazing at Your face;
to listen and learn from transforming truth
engulfed in seas of peace
drinking of Your grace.

How far distant the completion of time,
when mortal is swallowed
and all is made new?
Perfect fellowship at long last restored,
I'll wander in wonder
walking next to You.

Michael M. Middleton

from Sacred Journeys
Copyright 2002

Special Supplemental

The following special supplemental materials come from articles I originally wrote to use at a youth drop-in center which my wife and I pioneered with The Salvation Army in Klamath Falls, Oregon. I present them here for your enjoyment and enrichment. Permission is hereby granted to reproduce this portion of the book in whole or part for non-commercial purposes. Please feel free to utilize these resources in your personal or corporate ministry endeavors, noting the source.

What Kind Of Dirt Are You ?

In the Bible, Jesus tells a parable (picture story) about a farmer sowing seeds, which fall on different kinds of soil. (see Matthew 13: 3-23) Jesus says that the seed is the word of God; the very heart of which is the 'Gospel'; the good news that we can be saved. Saved from death; which each one of us deserves, because we have each, at some point, rebelled against God. God is the only source of life. So, if we turn our back on Him, we automatically choose death.

"For the wages of sin is death, but the gift of God is eternal life in Christ Jesus our Lord." (*Romans 6:23*)

"For God so loved the world that he gave His only begotten Son, that whoever believes in Him should not perish but have everlasting life. For God did not send His Son into the world to condemn the world, but that the world through Him might be saved." (*John 3:16-17*)

When the seed of God's word is sown, it falls on different kinds of soil… representing different kinds of people and the various ways they respond to its truths. Some people are 'hard'… hard - hearted and hard - headed ! Like rock hard soil, they refuse to allow a soft spot for the seed to take root. These people harden themselves against the love, forgiveness, and acceptance which God freely offers. They listen to Satan's deceptions and are robbed of eternal life.

Other people are like shallow soil. They get all excited about God at first, but since they have no "depth", no commitment to stick it out through tough times, they wither away at the first sign of difficulty. They were only in it for the "goodies" or the excitement of "trying something new". They are selfish, shallow people.

Next, there are those who are like soil filled with weeds and thorns. These "weeds" and "thorns" represent the entanglements and cares of the world... such things as greed, envy, materialism, paralyzing anxiety, and the many other "cares of the world". These choke out any true life by keeping their eyes and minds focused on problems and selfish pursuits instead of on God.

Finally, there are people who are like good soil; soft and receptive to truth, with a true heart commitment to love God and stick it out, even when things aren't rosy. These people choose to trust God with all of their cares, concerns, and needs. This is the soil which has real value and produces a valuable crop of a life well lived, which blesses God. In turn, these lives serve as a beacon to help guide others out of sin and death and into eternal life.

So, I ask you again, what kind of dirt are you ?

The Dirt - Simple Bible

God made man: "...so God made man in His own image; in the image of God He created him; male and female He created them." *Genesis 1:27*

Man screwed things up: "There is none righteous, not one...for all have sinned and fallen short of the glory of God." *Romans 3:10,23*

God fixed it: "...for God so loved the world that he gave His only begotten Son, that whoever believes in Him should not perish, but have everlasting life." *John 3:16*

"But He was wounded for our transgressions, He was bruised for our iniquities; the chastisement for our peace was upon Him, and by His stripes we are healed. All we like sheep have gone astray; we have turned, every one, to his own way; and the Lord has laid on Him the iniquity of us all." *Isaiah 53:5-6*

How do I get in on this ? : "...if you confess with your mouth the Lord Jesus and believe in your heart that God has raised Him from the dead, you will be saved...for 'whoever calls on the name of the Lord shall be saved.' " *Romans 10:9,13*

"He who covers his sins shall not prosper, but whoever confesses and forsakes them will have mercy." *Proverbs 28:13*

Can Robots Love ?
(considering evil and free will)

"If there really is a God, how can He allow such evil in the world ?"

When we daily hear of such evils as rape, murder, and child abuse… to say nothing of the atrocities of war, it's easy to ask this question. But, there is an answer:
FREE WILL.

God created man with free will; the ability to choose his actions for himself, be it good or evil. Why ? Because robots can't love. God created mankind for this one purpose: LOVE. Robots can't love; because love, by its very nature, must be a free - will choice.

"See, I have set before you today life and good, death and evil…" *Deuteronomy 30:15*

And then He leaves the choice up to us !

Just as a carpenter or other tradesman cannot fulfill his purpose without his tools; so we cannot fulfill our purpose, which is a relationship with a loving God, without using our tools of free will. But, just as a claw hammer can be used for evil, so can free will. Black and Decker is not at fault for making the hammer if someone uses it for evil. Neither is God at fault if we (or others) do evil… and each of us have !

"for ALL have sinned and fall short of the glory of God." *Romans 3:23* (emphasis mine.)

Darkness is a Biblical symbol for evil; and light, for good. We are told, "...God is Light and in Him is no darkness at all." *1John 1:5*

Reality check:

Don't let anyone ever talk you into thinking that if you become a Christian that everything will be sunshine and roses from that point on. Even when you are a committed child of God, those around you still have free will and some will do things to harm you. But, Christians have a hope that those in darkness do not have:

"And we know that ALL THINGS work together for good to those who love God, to those who are the called according to His purpose."
Romans 8:28 (emphasis mine)

Even when others purposely harm us, God uses it for good, in the big picture. I know that I can look back on some very painful times in my own life, and yet be grateful for God allowing me to go through those circumstances. I can honestly see how big of a jerk I'd still be, if I had not gone through some 'chastening'. If we stick close to God, we cannot help but win great victories, despite, or perhaps even because of, the fiery trials of life .

"Do not be overcome by evil, but overcome evil with good." *Romans 12:21*

Also, we who are Christians have a greater hope to come; a new home where evil has no place:

"And I saw a new heaven and a new earth, for the first heaven and the first earth had passed away. Also there was no more sea... And God will wipe away every tear from their eyes; there shall be no more death, nor sorrow, nor crying; and there shall be no more pain, for the former things have passed away." *Revelation 21:1,4*

Unfortunately, there is bad news for those who stubbornly reject God's love and choose evil. Time WILL, someday soon, run out. The books WILL be balanced !

"But the cowardly, unbelieving, abominable, murderers, sexually immoral, sorcerers, idolaters, and all liars shall have their part in the lake which burns with fire and brimstone, which is the second death."   *Revelation 21:8*

This is what we ALL deserve. We have ALL misused our free will. But God freely offers forgiveness and a restoration to the purpose for which He made us.

"If we confess our sins, He is faithful and just to forgive us our sins, and to cleanse us from all unrighteousness." *1John 1:9*

"He who covers his sins will not prosper, but whoever confesses and forsakes them will have mercy." *Proverbs 28:13*

Robots can't love, but you can.
What's your choice ?

Whada Ya' Mean "Born Again" ?

Have you ever heard someone talking about being "born again" ? Have you ever wondered what those nutty - sounding people were talking about? You are not alone.

Jesus once explained it to a confused fellow named Nicodemus like this:

"Most assuredly, I say to you, unless one is born again, he cannot see the kingdom of God...Most assuredly, I say to you, unless one is born of water and the Spirit, he cannot enter the Kingdom of God. That which is born of the flesh is flesh, and that which is born of the Spirit is spirit."
John 3:3, 5-6

Being 'born again' simply means turning control of your life over to the One who gave you life...Jesus Christ. Let's look at what that means <u>specifically;</u> which will help us understand why it's so important.

Lessons on anatomy they never taught in school:

God originally created man as a being in *three* parts...three parts distinct from one another; yet working in perfect harmony with each other. Surely, this is at least a hint at what God meant when He said that He created man "in His own image..." *(Genesis 1:27)* In mankind, these three parts are:

<u>Body:</u> The organic, physical body; created out of the elements of this earth (the dust of the ground) and forever linked to it.

Soul: The expression of the mind; emotions, will, memory, and thought… the home of both the intellectual and artistic in each of us.

Spirit: Who we really are. Spirit is the part of us that has its origin in another realm, another dimension. It was created in us by God to enable us to communicate with Him and to relate to him; because He is Spirit.(see *John 4:24*)

   The vast majority of us were born with a functioning body and mind ('soul'). But the fact is, unless you are a Christian, one third of YOU is dead, because of sin (turning your back on God, the source of life).

"…for all have sinned, and fall short of the glory of God…" *Romans 3:23*and we are told in *Romans 6:23,* " for the wages of sin is death…" ; death of the spirit immediately, the body to follow later. It's like being in a coma, of sorts. Machines can feed you and keep your body alive, but the brain is not functioning as it was meant to. The spiritual counterpart to this involves a functioning body and mind, but a "brain-dead spirit".

The cure: But, this 'coma of the spirit' is REVERSABLE. Your body has already been born; and your mind has developed along with it. Being 'born again' is really your spirit's first birth. If you are not now, as you read this, a Christian, your spirit lies dead within you; due to the sin charged atmosphere of planet Earth. You are unable to understand God in any measure, or make sense of His Word (the Bible) to any great degree, because the part of you that was designed for that purpose is not functioning. But, there is a way for your spirit to be made ALIVE. God is the creator and only source of life. He offers you life, in its fullest measure, through what Jesus did on our behalf. He took the penalty of our sins on Himself. He now offers you new life… eternal life… spiritual life.

The one and only way for you to receive this life if to accept what Jesus did on your behalf… and to give yourself fully to He who gave Himself fully for you. It's a lot like getting married: would you want your fiancé to only pledge 30% of their love and devotion ? Would you go through with the wedding? No-Way ! It's gotta' be 100% both ways.

Cut to the chase:

No matter how 'good' you have been, we all deserve death. (see *Romans 3:23*)

But, no matter how <u>bad</u> you've been, God loves you and wants to restore you to the purpose for which you were created.

" 'Come now, and let us reason together,' says the Lord. 'Though your sins are like scarlet, they shall be as white as snow; though they are red like crimson, they shall be as wool.' " *Isaiah 1:18*

"For God so loved the world, that he gave His only begotten Son, that whoever believes in him should not perish but have everlasting life. For God did not send His Son into the world to condemn the world, but that the world through Him might be saved." *John 3:16*

Whada Ya' Mean "SIN" ?

The most important and most basic choice we will make in this life is posed to us in the bible. In *Romans 6:23*, we read, "For the wages of sin is death, but the gift of God is eternal life in Christ Jesus our Lord."

Sin brings death. You might think,"…well, everybody's gonna' die !", but this scripture refers not only to physical death, but to spiritual death as well: an eternity separated from God in a place devoid of any goodness and any hope; a place of self imposed torment called "Hell".

You may believe that you are basically a good person and certainly can't have done anything deserving of Hell, but the Bible clearly states: "for all have sinned and fall short of the glory of God." (*Romans 3:23*) The noted physicist Albert Einstein taught us that all modes of measurement in the universe (speed, distance, mass; even color) are relative to the one observing any given object. Each man may look at himself and believe himself to be a basically good person; as he measures himself in relationship to those around him ("well, I'm not as bad as…"). But, when we are measured against the one supreme standard of the Universe… namely, it's creator, Jesus Christ… it is clear that we all fall miserably short. The Bible further states: "If we say that we have no sin, we deceive ourselves, and the truth is not in us." (*1John 1:8*)

Let's get specific...
So, if sin carries such a heavy price, just what exactly is it ? And, what about the sins we've already committed ? And, if 'nobody's perfect', what hope is there ?

Sin is often referred to as "missing the mark." It's very much like being in an archery contest... with your life depending on a perfect bull's-eye. You might think that you are a pretty good shot, but there are a few complicating factors: **1.** You're blindfolded. **2.** You've got a broken arm. **3.** All your arrows are crooked. Go ahead, take a shot... you'll miss the mark. Only a fool would think they had a chance in this situation.

The solution:
What Jesus did on our behalf was like Robin Hood showing up and offering to take the shot for us. You've only gotta' let go of your pride, admit that you cannot make the shot, and let Him do it on your behalf. In *John 14:6* Jesus said, "I am the way, the truth, and the life. No one comes to the Father (*and eternal life*) except through Me." Jesus is the only way for our sin debt to be paid, because He is the only one who does not owe that debt himself. All that He asks is that we admit our need, and allow Him to meet it.

"For He made Him who knew no sin to be sin for us, that we might become the righteousness of God in Him." (*2Corinthians 5:21*)

"If we confess our sins, He is faithful to forgive us our sins and to cleanse us from all unrighteousness." (*1John 1:9*)

Foundations of Faith

Faith is sometimes expressed in action when we see no need and have no desire to do what is directed by God; yes, even when it looks as though the doing will bring disaster upon us… and there is no way it can even possibly be done. This is akin to stepping off a cliff and trusting God to build a bridge under your feet, inch by inch, as you walk.

Faith is sometimes expressed through doing NOTHING, when it seems as though everything in your life is falling to pieces; as if you shall surely perish if you do not do something… anything to save yourself. It is remaining still in the midst of chaos, beholding God in His apparent inactivity (when it looks as though He doesn't even care) yet, trusting that he does care… and is in control.

In any situation, in either of these expressions, faith is the outworking of an individual's love for Father God and of their trust in His faultless character, which is incapable of harboring a single flaw. He is the ever-giving One… totally bereft of such base instincts as selfishness, envy, bitterness, or revenge. The all-powerful, all knowing, omnipresent, everlasting, CREATOR OF ALL is infinitely impotent in the traits of the fallen nature.

Oh, how unaware we are of how little faith we actually possess ! How totally oblivious are we to how little we actually trust the perfect expression of LOVE and faithfulness; the only true source of any good thing. How difficult it is for us to rely upon He who is most worthy of our trust; how easily we fear the One who is most benevolent towards us.

How totally unaware we are of the accusations towards God we harbor in our dark hearts. How many of us are willing to confess, even to ourselves, the suspicions and misplaced bitterness we aim at Him ?...

Our mouths say : *"Praise the Lord ! What a wonderful, faithful God !"*

While our hearts whisper : *(NO ! I cannot move ! He'll let me fall ! I must do something to save myself... He doesn't REALLY care about me...)*

With our mouths we proclaim : *"Praise God... He faithfully feeds His children ! "*

...Our dark hearts retort: *"Surely, He has given us bread, but can He give us meat as well ? "*

With love that surpasses any human reason or understanding, Father God releases harsh winds to buffet our pitiful frames. In great pain, He allows the flames of adversity and the ice of sorrow to pierce our hearts of stone. **He sees our innermost being continually.** He **continually** observes the bitterness, the suspicions, the faithlessness... the shriveled, putrid core of the fallen nature within us. It is we who are unaware of the death within us. He sees all, yet loves us not only for who we are now, but also for who we may become if we embrace His all encompassing mercy.

It is that mercy which allows circumstances into our lives which will reveal to us, in some small measure, how little we really love and trust Him. He never allows us to see the totality of our inner depravity; for that would destroy us. In patience and compassion, He shows us only enough of our inner darkness to shock us into reality; to drive us to our knees to seek His face. He feels our pain more than we; yet, He endures it in foreknowledge that it is necessary to our healing. If we do not witness the reality of our inner darkness, we shall never turn from it to embrace the light.

Other books by

Michael M. Middleton:

Sacred Journeys

Modern Musings

Whispers of the Divine

*Available to order online,
or through your favorite bookstore.*

Also, see
www.Zazzle.com/Mgifts

Made in the USA
Charleston, SC
13 July 2012